LOVE MATCH

Also by Keira Andrews

Contemporary

Honeymoon for One
Beyond the Sea
Ends of the Earth
Arctic Fire
The Chimera Affair

Holiday
Only One Bed
Merry Cherry Christmas
The Christmas Deal
Santa Daddy
In Case of Emergency
Eight Nights in December
If Only in My Dreams
Where the Lovelight Gleams
Gay Romance Holiday Collection

Sports
Kiss and Cry
Reading the Signs
Cold War
The Next Competitor
Love Match
Synchronicity (free read!)

Gay Amish Romance Series
A Forbidden Rumspringa
A Clean Break
A Way Home
A Very English Christmas

Valor Duology
Valor on the Move
Test of Valor
Complete Valor Duology

Lifeguards of Barking Beach
Flash Rip
Swept Away (free read!)

Historical

Kidnapped by the Pirate
Semper Fi
The Station
Voyageurs (free read!)

Paranormal

Kick at the Darkness
Kick at the Darkness
Fight the Tide

Taste of Midnight (free read!)

Fantasy

Barbarian Duet
Wed to the Barbarian
The Barbarian's Vow

LOVE MATCH

BY KEIRA ANDREWS

Love Match
Written and published by Keira Andrews
Cover by Dar Albert
Formatting by BB eBooks

Second Edition

Copyright © 2021 by Keira Andrews
Print Edition
First Edition Published 2006

ISBN: 978-1-988260-58-7

Author's Note

I'm delighted to publish this 15th anniversary edition of *Love Match*. This was my first novel, originally released in 2006 by now-defunct press Loose Id. When I regained the publishing rights a few years ago, I decided I should edit and revise Luke and Jesse's story since surely I could improve on my first book.

Other projects have kept me busy, and when I finally sat down to reread this story, I discovered I like it just the way it is. Some references are dated, and I think attitudes toward gay athletes have come a long way. I'd certainly write it differently today—though as of 2021 there has still never been an openly LGBTQ+ male tennis player at the elite level. And while I'm always striving to grow as a writer, we could spend the rest of our lives endlessly editing and looking backward if we're not careful!

Love Match was the first step in my dream career as a romance author, and I'm excited to have Luke and Jesse back out in the world instead of collecting dust. I hope you enjoy this story of finding love and being true to yourself while winning tennis matches along the way.

Keira

<3

CHAPTER ONE

2006

"OUT!"

The linesman's voice rang across the court, and Steve Anderson sat up straighter in the announcer's booth.

Luke Rossovich swore and tossed down his racquet. After a few more expletives, he strode to the umpire's chair, hands on hips. He peered up into the punishing Australian sun. "That ball was good. I know it, you know it, and everyone in this stadium except that linesman knows it." The crowd hooted and hollered.

Steve and his fellow commentator grinned at each other. "Let's go to the replay and see if Rossovich has reason for complaint. The ball looked like it might have been good to me, but our Court Cam will tell us for sure," Steve said.

As the umpire tried to mollify the angry player, the home audience saw the ball catching the outside of the line. "Yep, that ball was good," Steve confirmed. "But looks like Rossovich isn't going to win this argument—the umpire isn't going to overrule on such a close call. I know how he feels; I lost a few of those calls myself over the years." Steve had been a decent player who had lucked into a Wimbledon championship one year when the top seeds were all eliminated early. He was milking that win for all it was worth, commentating for American TV and endorsing cheap tennis balls.

"This is bullshit!" Luke finally turned and stalked back to where his racquet laid on the court. His opponent, a young Swede, waited on the other side of the net. With the bad call, the Swede now had break point to win the set. Luke picked up his racquet and promptly threw it again, the cracking of the frame audible to everyone in attendance.

"Rossovich just cost himself the first set!" Steve exclaimed. "He threw his racquet hard enough to break it, and that's definitely going to be a point against him. This kind of temper tantrum is something we haven't seen from Ross in a few years, and it couldn't have come at a worse time."

"Point Penalty to Rossovich. Grankvist wins the first set, 6-4."

Steve shook his head and whistled. "This just might not be Luke Rossovich's day."

LUKE TIPPED HIS head back, his eyes closed as the water cascaded down his body. His muscles ached and the joint in his knee was uncomfortably stiff. He tried to lose himself in the hot shower, tried to let go of his spectacularly shitty day.

"Fuck!" He slapped the tile wall. It was no use. He'd lost in the second round of the Australian Open. The second goddamned round. At thirty-four, he sure as hell wasn't getting many more chances, and he'd blown this one but good.

"Tough break today."

Luke opened his eyes and peered through the steam. A young blond man turned on the water a few showers down. Luke thought for a few seconds and remembered his name and bio. Jesse McAllister: twenty-three years old, NCAA champion out of UCLA. Had cracked the top one hundred in the world after his first two years on tour, which wasn't bad. Still, he was supposed to have been America's great new hope, and so far he hadn't quite lived up to expectations.

"Yeah. You could say that." Luke wasn't really in the mood for small talk.

Jesse opened a bottle of shampoo and lathered his hair. "You know, you should play more doubles. Your net game is suffering a bit."

"Oh, really?" The nerve of this...*kid* coming in here and offering *him* advice.

"I just noticed that your volleys are pretty flat." Luke was glad to hear a note of nervousness in the kid's voice.

"Well, they weren't too bad when I won Wimbledon. Three times. Not to mention this tournament once." Granted, that was four years ago now.

Jesse rinsed the shampoo out of his hair and turned the water off. "No argument here. Look, I was just wondering if maybe you wanted to play doubles at Indian Wells. I think our games would mesh really well. But forget it." He slung his towel around his slim hips. He was around five foot seven and slight, but toned and in great shape. He didn't have a power game, but if Luke recalled correctly, he made up for it with his speed. "See ya."

Then he was gone and Luke closed his eyes again, wishing he could just be home in his bed in Malibu. Instead, he had yet another hotel room to go to, with an ugly duvet and nouveau art on the wall that was all the same, no matter which city he was in. He sighed and turned the water up hotter.

THE AIRPORT LOUNGE was packed, and Luke pulled his baseball cap down further over his brown hair. Mirrored sunglasses hid his green eyes, and as he folded his long, lean frame into a chair, he hoped no one would recognize him. He wasn't in the mood to put on a smile and sign autographs. But at six feet, two inches, with a taut, finely muscled body and a face that *People* had called "movie-star handsome" on more than one occasion, Luke tended to stick out in a crowd.

The Aussies were huge tennis fans, so the tournament played on every available TV screen, much to Luke's dismay. He just wanted to forget about this particular competition and look towards the next Grand Slam event, the French Open. He didn't have much of a shot of winning it, but stranger things had happened.

Luke still had almost an hour to kill, so his gaze inevitably drifted to the closest screen. He felt a strange little jolt when he recognized the player in the far court. Jesse McAllister's blond hair was practically glowing in the sun, sweat dripping down his brow. He'd made it to the third round but was now playing one of the top seeds. He was down two sets and a break. It wasn't looking good. Once a player had lost a game he was serving, his serve was "broken." Since a set must be won by two games, the other player gained the advantage.

Jesse managed to break back to even the set, and Luke found himself getting more and more involved in the match. Jesse played with a grace that many compared to Bjorn Borg, and what he lacked in power, he made up for with finesse. The kid was right—their games *would* mesh well.

As Jesse toweled off during a changeover, Luke's boarding call crackled over the loudspeakers. Onscreen, Jesse pulled his shirt over his head, his lightly tanned chest glistening.

Twenty minutes later, Jesse lost the match in a third-set tie-break, and Luke sprinted to make his flight.

Once the plane was in the air, Luke tried to relax. Thankfully, the seat next to his in first class was empty, so he didn't need to make small talk. He watched a movie and picked at his dinner. Eventually he popped a couple of heavy-duty sleeping pills and didn't wake up again until the California coast was in sight.

The traffic out of LAX was terrible, but that was nothing new.

The driver looked in his rearview mirror often and tried to engage Luke in conversation. He was cute enough, and Luke thought briefly about telling him to pull over and join him in the backseat once they reached the quiet, hilly back roads near his house. As usual, the words just wouldn't come. He needed a shower and a drink. Not necessarily in that order.

The house smelled stale, although the maid had clearly been by that morning to spruce things up. Cut flowers graced his kitchen table and the fridge contained all his favorite foods.

Luke opened a beer and walked out onto his deck. The sun had set, the quarter moon casting only a little light on the waves he could hear lapping at the beach in the distance. His pool and tennis court lay below, both immaculately kept.

He took a swig of beer and sighed. Tomorrow it would all start again, the inexorable push towards the next tournament. He'd practice and prepare and would probably lose early on, if his recent luck held. The thought flitted through his mind again— maybe it was time for a coach. He hadn't had one for two years now.

At the thought, pain blossomed in his chest, regular as clock-work.

He slammed the rest of his beer back and headed upstairs. His bedroom was large, with French doors that opened onto a balcony that overlooked the sea. Luke shut the drapes and took another sleeping pill, hoping he wouldn't dream.

He tossed and turned for hours, strange images flitting through his mind, keeping him on the edges of real rest.

In the morning, his trainer Aaron arrived on schedule at seven. Luke was jet-lagged and irritable; they hardly spoke as they jogged on the beach before starting drills. Drills were the same as ever: First his backhand, then his forehand, then his serve.

"I should work on my volleys," Luke said as Aaron refilled the tennis ball machine.

"Your volleys? What for? You come into net about once a millennium these days."

"Well, maybe I should change that."

Aaron opened his arms wide, displaying the muscles he spent hours a day in the gym maintaining. "You're the boss." He grinned, the dimple in his cheek matching the twinkle in his eyes.

For the next few hours, Luke charged the net repeatedly. After what was probably his twentieth missed volley, he cursed Jesse McAllister for ever opening his big mouth.

LUKE'S FOREHAND SAILED long and his racquet thudded to the ground. It had been a week and his net game was still pathetic. The rest of his shots weren't too hot either, and frustration was setting in.

"Hey, don't work yourself too hard," Luke's hitting partner, Mike Madison, said as he approached. "Look, I know you must be upset about the Aussie and about Alexandra, but give yourself a break, buddy."

Luke took a gulp of water and nodded. Then his brow creased in confusion. "Wait, what about Alexandra? I haven't talked to her in forever."

Mike blanched. "Shit, I thought you knew. She married that racecar driver over the weekend in Monaco. They kept it a pretty good secret until afterwards."

Well, well, Alex had finally landed a dream husband. "Oh. Good for her, I guess." The "relationship" between Alex and Luke had only been one of mutual convenience. Her days as a top supermodel were over, and being with Luke had kept her in the spotlight. They had seen each other only a few times a year but always made sure the paparazzi were on hand to take plenty of pictures.

After Luke's career had dipped, she'd informed him that she was moving on. Luke played the heartbroken ex-boyfriend very successfully, and no one bothered him about his love life. Which was fine by him.

"Sorry, man. I know it still gets to you." Mike clapped Luke on the back. "Come on, let's call it a day and go grab a brew."

Luke nodded and they headed to the players' lounge in the club. Oceanside Tennis Club was just down the street from his house in Malibu, and Luke and Mike met regularly to hit with each other, as they did on tour. Without a coach, Luke needed someone to practice with, and Mike was easygoing and a good friend. A journeyman who'd never made it to the top of the game and never would, Mike kept slogging away year after year, making a living. At thirty-five, he was close to hanging up his racquet on the tour.

Naturally, the Australian Open played on the big-screen TV in the lounge. The German who had beaten Jesse McAllister, Stein Koehler, was on court playing for the championship.

"Did you see him play against that kid from UCLA in the third round? What's his name? McAllister?" Luke tried to keep his voice casual.

Mike nodded as he stretched his arms over his head. He was an inch taller than Luke and well muscled, with close-cropped brown hair and a warm, open face. "Yeah, McAllister had a good third set, took him to a breaker. He just might follow your example and start winning Slams. But so far he never seems to be able to put it together when it counts."

"He's got the talent."

"Yeah. You know, I hear he's going to be playing out of Brookview again; he fired his coach in Florida and he's moving back to LA."

"Huh." Luke sipped his beer and munched on a pretzel.

Mike looked at his watch and groaned. "I'd better get going, or Shelley will have my hide. I have to help Tara with her math homework or I'm in trouble. See you tomorrow."

"Have a good one. And hey, tell Shell to stop feeding you so well—you're getting a bit thick around the middle."

"Yeah, yeah." Mike laughed, playfully punching Luke in the shoulder as he left.

Luke ordered another beer and finished watching the match. He tried not to think about the fact that it should be him on court, the hot sun beating down, another title within his grasp.

"BROOKVIEW GOLF AND Country Club. How may I help you?" The young woman's voice was crisp and pleasant.

"I'm trying to reach Jesse McAllister. I believe he's going to be practicing at your tennis club again." Luke's throat was strangely dry. Why the hell was he doing this? He should just forget Jesse and focus on his training.

The woman hesitated. "I might be able to pass on a message."

"It's Luke Rossovich calling."

"*The* Luke Rossovich? The tennis player?"

"The one and only." Luke applied his practiced charm and could practically hear the woman's composure melt.

"Oh my god, you were totally amazing the first time you won Wimbledon. And the second! Not to mention the third, of course! I'm such a big fan!"

"Thank you very much. What's your name?"

"Amber."

"Well, Amber, if you can get me Jesse McAllister's number, I'll be sure to send you an autographed picture."

"Really? That would be so awesome," she gushed. "Okay, just a second." She put him on hold and was back in a minute with the number. She also gave him *her* phone number, along with her home address. Luke promised to send the picture soon and made a note to do it later. A promise was a promise, after all.

As he dialed Jesse's number, he felt strangely nervous. It rang, and he considered hanging up, but then Jesse was speaking. "Hey, it's Jesse. Blah, blah, blah, leave a message."

Suddenly Luke was stammering into the phone. "Uh, it's Luke Rossovich. I was thinking about what you said in Melbourne. Maybe it's not a bad idea, playing doubles. I could teach you a thing or two. Call me back if you're into it."

He winced. *Into it?* He sounded like a teenager. He flopped down on the couch and turned on the TV, flipping the channels aimlessly until he settled on a rerun of a cop show he'd probably seen before.

When the phone rang, Luke jerked upright. He'd dozed off and he shook his head to try to clear the cobwebs. His stomach lurched when he saw Jesse's name on the call display. Jesus, he really *was* acting like a teenager—what was it about this kid?

"Hello?"

"Luke? It's Jesse McAllister."

"Hey. How's it going?"

"Fine. I still have to finish unpacking and stuff. I hate moving."

"Yeah, it sucks." For some strange reason, Luke couldn't think of anything else to say.

"So, um…you want to give it a try?"

"Huh?" Luke's pulse suddenly increased.

"Doubles. Playing together. That's why you called, right?"

Yes, yes, that was why he'd called. "Right. Let's give it a shot."

"You free on Saturday? I could meet you at your club. You're in Malibu, right?"

"Yeah. But you can come to my place if you want. I have a court. It's quieter here."

"Okay, sounds good."

Luke gave him the address and they arranged a time. After he hung up, Jesse's "See ya," rang in his ears. He picked up the remote and started flipping through the channels again, a smile tugging at his lips.

CHAPTER TWO

J ESSE LUNGED, HIS arm outstretched. His racquet barely caught the ball and sent it flying up into the air and out of bounds.

"Man, that's one hell of a rocket you've got," he said, shaking his head.

Luke grinned. "You're damn right. Used to be the fastest serve on the ATP until Riel came along."

"I guess that's the problem, huh? Always someone younger and better nipping at your heels." Jesse wiped his forehead with his sleeve. It was a cool day, but they were working up a sweat.

"Yeah. Such is life, I suppose." Luke served again, and Jesse got a good look at it, smacking a winner up the line.

They had decided to play against each other for a while before they tried working on the same side. He was impressed with Jesse's game, and for the first time in a good long while, Luke was actually having *fun* playing tennis.

They rallied back and forth and went to a first-set tiebreaker. Luke won it, but just barely. In the second set, Luke played a couple of loose points and Jesse wound up with the break and the set.

"Winner takes all in the third?" Jesse asked.

"Sounds like a plan."

They both took a minute to towel off and drink some of the energy juice Luke kept in a cooler at the side of the court. He tried not to stare as Jesse poured some water over his head, shaking his hair like a dog. The water glistened in fat drops on the blond strands, some dripping down his face in long rivulets. Luke licked his lips unconsciously.

Jesse looked at him and blinked, his blue eyes piercing. "What?"

Luke snapped to attention. "What?"

"That's what I said." Jesse smiled.

"Huh?"

"Oh, never mind. Let's play!" Jesse jogged back to the other side of the court, where he bobbed side to side on his toes.

"You sure you're ready for the rocket?" Luke called.

"Bring it!" Jesse yelled back.

They played on, both grunting with exertion as they ran around the court, pounding groundstrokes back and forth. Luke finally got the break and won the set. He pumped his fist as he moved towards the net. Even though it wasn't a real competition, they both walked towards each other automatically to shake hands.

"I'll beat you next time." Jesse grinned.

"That's what they all say, kid."

They clasped palms and Luke's heart skipped a beat, a tingle moving up his arm as if he'd just touched a light socket. He pulled his hand away and smiled nervously. Okay, this was getting ridiculous.

"So, wanna set up the ball machine and play on the same side of the net?" Jesse asked.

"Sure."

They each played a side of the court, and often ended up chasing after the same balls. After a narrowly missed collision, Jesse called a time-out.

"When was the last time you played doubles?"

"Uh…a while ago." Luke hadn't played doubles professionally

since he was just starting on the tour. He'd played for fun sometimes, but then…then everything had changed.

"Obviously. You can't keep going after my balls, Luke."

Luke's throat went dry, and he nearly choked. "What?"

"If a ball comes down the middle, one of us calls it and the other backs off, okay? You do remember the basics, I presume?"

Luke nodded. "Right. Sorry."

"It's okay. You seem a little tense. You all right?"

"Yep. Just a bit rusty at this." Understatement of the year.

"No problem. Just follow my lead." Jesse smiled.

Luke couldn't help but notice how Jesse's smile lit up his whole face, and it made Luke smile in return every time.

He nodded, and followed.

WHEN THE PHONE rang later that night, Luke was flipping channels, still unable to find anything that could hold his interest for more than a few seconds.

"Hello?"

"Ross! How ya doing?"

Luke sighed. He wasn't really in the mood. "Hey, Arnie."

"I'm great, thanks for asking." Arnie Lachance was Luke's agent, the man who had won Luke so many millions in endorsements over the years that Luke never needed to hit a tennis ball again to make money.

"Glad to hear it. What's up?"

"They want you to come play an exhibition in South America next week. Just show up, play one match, and a big fat check will be waiting in your bank account."

"I don't know, Arnie. I'm kind of busy."

"Busy? What are you busy with that I don't know about?"

Luke sighed. "It's nothing involving money, so I'm sure you

wouldn't be interested."

"Well, if it's going to stop you from playing this match, you can bet your sweet ass I'm interested."

"I'm just playing doubles. Trying to get my net game back into shape."

"*Doubles?*" Arnie's voice dripped with disdain. "There's no money in doubles. Hell, there's not even glory. What the fuck's the point?"

"The point is to improve my game so I can win the big money tournaments again."

"Ahhh, now you're talking."

Luke snorted. "Somehow I knew that would get through to you."

"Come on, you can still do this exhibition. They love you Down Under."

"South America is not Down Under, Arnie. That's Australia."

"Wherever. You're huge with these people."

"So huge that they're asking me a week before the event?"

Arnie was silent for a moment, and Luke could practically hear the wheels in motion. "Well, you see—"

"Who backed out?"

"What? Don't be crazy. You're their first choice, Ross."

"Mm-hmm. Let me guess, Koehler dropped out. Or maybe Castillo."

"Okay, so Castillo just twisted his ankle. Hey, maybe he'll be out for the French, too. That wouldn't be a bad thing."

"Arnie, it's going to take more than a Spaniard's twisted ankle for me to win the French."

The French Open was the only Grand Slam played on red clay, which slowed the ball down and took away the advantage of the big power servers. Champions at Roland Garros in Paris duked it out from the base line, and often the victors came from Spain or South America, countries where clay courts were common.

"Hey, what's with that attitude? Come on, Ross, you've still got a Slam left in you. I know it."

Luke knew Arnie's interest in him would only last as long as the endorsements did, but at least he believed in him. "Thanks, Arn. Sure, tell them I'll be there."

"You won't regret it, Luke. Hey, who're you playing doubles with?"

"Oh, you probably don't know him. Jesse McAllister." A ridiculous blush crept up Luke's neck.

"Sure, sure, blond kid out of UCLA. He coulda been a contender, but it looks like he ain't got the chops."

Luke felt a surge of irritation. "Yes, he does. He just hasn't quite put it together yet. A bit early to be writing him off."

"Well, tell him time's wasting. Speaking of time, I gotta jet. I'll fax the contract for South America over. Be sure to wear the new shirt Top Spin made for you. You got the shipment, right?"

Luke glanced over at the large box in the corner, still unopened. "Yeah, no problem. Okay, talk to you later."

He hung up and rummaged around in the fridge, finally deciding on some leftover pizza. He could never eat the stuff cold, so while it nuked, he paced idly in the kitchen, thinking about earlier, about playing with Jesse. When the microwave beeped, Luke shook his head and swore that he wouldn't think about Jesse McAllister again for the rest of the day.

He lasted all of five minutes.

TRAFFIC AT LAX was just as bad going in as coming out. Luke checked his watch repeatedly, even though he was still early enough to make his flight in plenty of time. The driver barely looked at him, just whistled along to a song Luke didn't recognize on the radio.

He and Jesse had practiced together once more on the weekend, and Luke felt like they were getting into a pretty good rhythm. There was only one near-collision, and Luke had to admit that he didn't really mind getting close to Jesse when the opportunity arose.

But he was being absurd.

He knew nothing could ever come of it. For starters, Jesse was eleven years his junior. So what if Jesse made him laugh, *really* laugh, for the first time in a long time? There was no way anything could ever happen. Luke couldn't get close to anyone again—it just wasn't possible.

Besides, Jesse probably wasn't even gay.

Well, okay, he totally was. He'd never said as much, but Luke's gaydar was pretty finely honed. He suspected there were a few other closet cases on the tour—statistically speaking there had to be—and now he was sure Jesse was one of them. Not that they'd ever talk about it.

The pro tennis tour was still a bastion of old-fashioned macho male egos and swagger—definitely not an environment in which gays found a welcome. The women's tour had its fair share of lesbians, many of them successful and beloved by fans. However, no male tennis pro had ever come out on the tour. Rumors surrounded the odd player over the years, but those rumors had never been substantiated.

Luke's cell phone rang, shaking him from his reverie. "Hello?"

"Luke. It's Jesse."

"Oh, hey." Luke's pulse increased and he rolled his eyes at himself. "What's up?"

"I just wanted to catch you before your flight. We're still on for Tuesday, right?"

"Yeah, sure. Unless something's come up?"

"No, no. I just wanted to make sure. I have to take my sister out for her birthday, and I wanted to make sure Tuesday was still okay."

"We can switch days, if you want."

"No, Tuesday's good."

"Okay."

"Okay."

Silence stretched out between them until Luke cleared his throat, "So…was there something else on your mind?"

"Oh, no, sorry. Have a good flight! Have fun in Santiago. Hope you win."

"I get the same amount of money either way."

"Well, still. Hope you win."

"Yeah, me too. Thanks. I'll see you Tuesday."

Luke snapped his phone shut. Why did it feel like he'd just made a date?

CHAPTER THREE

★★★ ★★★

THE RESTAURANT SERVED Chilean food, of course. Luke sat around a table with the organizers of the event and nodded and smiled at the appropriate moments. He'd played this part thousands of times before and knew exactly how to give people what they wanted.

The exhibition was a breeze, as his competitor was totally off his stride. Luke let him win a few games just to give the crowd a match that wasn't a complete blowout. After the match, Luke smiled and waved and signed hundreds of autographs with a shiny black marker, his own face staring back at him from glossy pages.

"So, Luke. How long are you planning on playing before you retire?" The woman, Gabrielle, was one of the event marketers. She'd been inching her leg closer to his all throughout dinner.

"Well, I guess I'll keep playing until my body says it doesn't want to anymore." The truth was his body told him that almost every morning, his muscles and joints stiff in a way they never were ten years ago.

"It's four years since you won a Slam. Think you have it in you for another? You must want the U.S. Open pretty badly. You came so close that year."

If she thought discussing his crushing past failures was the way to get him into bed, she was sorely mistaken. Not that she'd be getting him into bed anyway, for obvious reasons. "Yeah, I was pretty close."

"Do you still think about it? That one shot that went out on match point? A few inches, and you could have won."

Everyone at the table looked at him eagerly, as if they were hoping he was about to start crying. "Nah, I don't think about the past very much." Luke took another mouthful of the dish on his plate. Tasted like typical mashed potatoes to him.

They all nodded and looked slightly disappointed.

It was a lie, of course. Luke thought about that shot almost every day. He didn't mean to, but the linesman's voice echoed in his brain at the most inconvenient of times. He'd be at the grocery store, deciding on which high-fiber cereal sounded the least disgusting, when he'd hear the call.

A few inches, and he would have won. Would have been U.S. Open champion, would have won the three Grand Slams he had a real chance at. The French was probably never going to happen, and he could live with that. Sampras never won it, and he was an all-time great. However, not winning the U.S. was something that Luke struggled with.

Especially after coming so very, very close.

After Luke's missed match point, his serve had been soft and his opponent had won the advantage. The point after that, the game. Then they were into a tiebreaker. Luke lost, 7-9. He accepted the runner-up trophy and his check for hundreds of thousands of dollars, thanked the crowd and his opponent, and vowed to be back the next year.

It was two months later to the day that vows didn't matter anymore.

Luke hadn't really ever been back since. In body, maybe, but not in mind and spirit, not in the form that would allow him to get close to winning again. He wasn't sure he'd ever get it back.

After dinner, Gabrielle somehow ended up with him in the hotel elevator. Luke smiled politely. "Which floor?" His finger hovered over the elevator panel.

She looked at him coyly from under her thick eyelashes and tossed her glossy brown hair over her shoulder. "You tell me," she purred.

He smiled tightly. "I have an early flight in the morning. So, which floor is it?"

"Now, now, Luke, don't be such a spoilsport." She sidled closer and ran her hand up his chest, her long red nails tapping the buttons of his shirt. "Sleep is so overrated."

He punched the button for his floor and removed her hand. "Not for a professional athlete. Sorry. Maybe next time." His smile was cold, and she took a step back. At his floor, he exited with a polite good night and she didn't argue. He heard her huff as the doors slid shut.

In his room, Luke took off his suit and hung it carefully in a garment bag. With plenty of time, Luke polished his shoes before packing them as well. When there was nothing left to do, he lay down on the bed and tried to find something on TV in English.

Eventually he gave up and turned off the lights, shutting his eyes and willing his brain to stop thinking. To stop imagining a certain blond with a tight little body and a big smile. A mouth that could probably do some pretty amazing things—

"Christ," Luke groaned. He gave up and reached into his briefs, stroking his cock. He squeezed tightly and moved his fist up and down, imagining it was Jesse's hand, imagining that it was his mouth. He thought about how Jesse's body would feel beneath him, how his skin would taste.

Luke's hips lifted from the mattress and he planted his feet on the bed for more leverage as he worked himself. One hand found his nipples, teasing and pinching them as he jerked his dick hard—once, twice, three times before he came with a strangled moan.

His legs flopped down to the mattress, and he caught his

breath before he finally dragged himself to the bathroom to clean up. Soon, he was in a deep sleep, interrupted only by his wake-up call from the front desk.

"DID YOU REALLY have to bring the heat back with you from Chile?" Jesse fanned his face with his racquet.

"I thought it was the least I could do; it was threatening to snow last week." Luke smacked the ball over the net and waited for Jesse's return shot. The sun was high in the sky and only a faint breeze wafted over from the sea. It was February, but the temperature had soared into the high eighties.

"Har, har." Jesse hit a backhand cross-court.

Luke returned it, and they kept the rally going for another few shots before Luke hit a winner up the line. Out of breath, Luke pulled his tank top off over his head, tired of the cloth sticking to him.

"Good idea." Jesse followed suit, tossing his shirt to the side of the court.

Luke watched for a few moments: Jesse's firm stomach and lean arms, skin that looked smooth to the touch …

"—waiting for?"

"Huh?" Luke blinked. Jesse was staring at him.

"I said, what are you waiting for? It's your serve."

"Right." He served quickly, trying to avoid any further conversation. They rallied back and forth again, with Jesse eventually hitting a solid backhand into the corner. Luke saw it coming and tapped a drop shot just over the net. Jesse ran for it, legs flying, a blur of motion.

Just when Luke thought he was actually going to be able to return the shot, Jesse doubled over in pain, his racquet clattering to the ground as he fell. Luke was around the net before he'd even had a chance to think about it.

"Are you okay?" He kneeled beside Jesse on the hot surface of the court.

Jesse grimaced, his hands on his left leg. "It's just a cramp. I guess I'm not used to the heat right now."

"Here." Luke moved Jesse's hands aside and started kneading the stiff muscles.

"It's okay, I'll be fine," Jesse gritted out.

"Just sit there and shut up."

Jesse didn't argue, and Luke continued massaging his leg. He didn't apply too much pressure, just enough to dissipate some of the tension. He moved his hands over Jesse's calf and up to his thigh and tried not to think about how the skin was just as smooth as he thought it would be.

The fine blond hair on Jesse's legs felt soft under Luke's fingers as he kneaded and urged away any tightness. Neither of them spoke, and Luke could feel Jesse's breath on his cheek, could feel the heat from his body.

Suddenly it seemed like the air was electric, like there was nothing else in the world but the two of them. Nothing but the feel of Jesse's hot skin, the sound of his breathing. Luke felt a rush of blood to his cock when he noticed that Jesse was getting hard beneath his nylon shorts. He would only need to move his hand a few inches up Jesse's thigh and he could hold him, stroke him—

With a rush of air, Jesse's lips were on his, soft and hot and pressing insistently.

Luke jolted away as if Jesse had slapped him.

He sat back and sucked a deep breath into his lungs. He hadn't kissed anyone in a very long time, and he hadn't expected it to feel like this. He wasn't sure if he was so shocked because it was different from what he remembered, or because it was the same.

"I'm sorry!" Jesse jumped to his feet with a stricken expression on his face and hurried away, hobbling on his cramped leg before

Luke could even process what was happening.

"Jesse, wait. Look, I—"

It was no use. Jesse had broken out into an ungainly run, surely ignoring the pain in his muscles as he dashed up the stairs. Luke couldn't seem to move, and soon Jesse was out of sight around the house. His car roared to life and zoomed away into the hills.

He wasn't sure how long he sat there, but Luke finally got up and picked up their equipment, placing Jesse's racquet carefully back in its case. He was about to go inside when he noticed Jesse's shirt still lying by the court. The cotton was damp, and Luke held it to his face for a long moment before trudging back up the stairs to his empty house.

CHAPTER FOUR

THE SAND WAS hard beneath his feet, packed down by the unrelenting rain. The heat wave was over and Luke was glad; he welcomed the chill in the air, on his skin. He and Aaron raced alongside the waves, ignoring the rain that pelted them.

Luke ran hard, his chest burning by the time they reached the turnaround point at a cove up the coast. They headed back towards Luke's house, feet flying. With a burst of energy, Aaron sprang forwards, challenging Luke to keep up.

Luke increased his stride, pumped his arms faster as he nipped at Aaron's heels. Suddenly a stitch tore through Luke's side and he doubled over, hands on his knees.

"You okay?" Aaron jogged back to him.

Luke nodded and tried to take a deep breath. "I'm fine," he wheezed.

Aaron tilted his head and looked at him contemplatively. "You've seemed kind of off this week. Distracted. Everything okay?"

"Yeah, everything's fine." Luke stood up straight and started walking, wiping the rain off his face even though it was a losing battle.

Everything was far from fine. It had been three days, and all he could think about was Jesse. Jesse's laugh, Jesse's smile, Jesse's mouth.

"Jesus!" Luke laughed out loud. He sounded like some lovestruck teenager. It was insane.

"What?" Aaron waited patiently as the rain continued to pour down.

"Nothing. Forget it."

Aaron moved around in front of Luke, forcing him to stop. "Look, how many years have I been your trainer?"

Luke sighed. "Too many years."

"Don't I know it. And I know when something's up. So just get it off your chest already."

"There's nothing to tell."

Aaron crossed his arms. "I can wait all day. I'm on the clock, after all."

"I pay you to keep me in shape, not for therapy," Luke scoffed.

Aaron just watched him, unmoving. "I'm waiting."

"It's nothing." Luke rolled his eyes and mumbled, "Just some guy."

A grin broke out across Aaron's face. "Well, it's about time!"

"Like I said, it's nothing." Luke scowled, suddenly feeling very exposed. "Don't get all excited."

Aaron clapped a hand on Luke's shoulder. "Look, I know the past few years haven't been easy for you." He squeezed his fingers. "You never talk about what happened—"

"Because there's nothing to talk about." Luke shrugged away and started down the beach again at a jog.

"Come on, man," Aaron said as he caught up. "It's great that you met someone new."

"I told you it's nothing. Don't act like I found a replacement."

"Hey, no one said anything about that. Luke, no one's ever going to replace him."

"Yeah, no shit." Luke sped up, despite the pain in his side.

"But you being alone and miserable isn't going to bring him

back."

Luke ran faster, and Aaron let him go. The waves pounded the beach, the rain falling harder. Luke's eyes burned and he blinked rapidly, his tears quickly washed away.

THAT NIGHT, LUKE tried to think of something other than Jesse and the look on his face after Luke had pushed him away. He knew pain when he saw it, and guilt gnawed away at him until he picked up the phone.

It took another ten minutes to actually dial all the numbers, and as the phone rang, Luke thought about hanging up. There was no answer, and he couldn't think of anything to say on voicemail that wouldn't sound pathetic.

The next day, Luke got into his SUV and drove to the other side of the city. He went to a special health food store that stocked some Asian herbs that promised to increase his energy and sharpen his mind. So what if that health food store happened to be near the Brookview Golf and Country Club?

It was an hour out of his way, but Luke couldn't stand the silence anymore. Granted, the silence was his fault. Therefore, it was about time he did something about it.

The lobby of the club was ornate and polished, standard-issue playground of the rich and famous. When Luke was growing up in Orange County, he never thought he'd end up in places like this. He approached the receptionist, whose eyes lit up as she saw him.

"Oh my god, Luke Rossovich! Hi, I'm Amber. We spoke on the phone a couple of weeks ago. I got your picture in the mail. I can't thank you enough!"

Luke smiled with practiced ease. "My pleasure, Amber. Hey, which court is Jesse McAllister playing on?"

Amber checked a schedule on her desk. "Oh, he's over on court number two. Do you know the way? I can show you—"

"No, that's okay. I know the way." He smiled again before hurrying off.

Jesse was nowhere to be found, and Luke eventually tried the locker room. He spotted a flash of blond hair, and his mouth went dry as he saw Jesse, naked except for the towel he was drying his back with. His ass was high and round and damn spectacular. Luke thought about what it would be like to—

"Hey, aren't you Luke Rossovich?"

"Huh? Yeah, yeah I am." Luke cleared his throat and stuck his hand out to the man who had just entered the locker room. They shook hands and made small talk while Jesse, who had whirled around when he heard Luke's name, yanked on his clothes as fast as possible. Luke watched him from the corner of his eye, and finally his admirer went on his way.

"Jesse."

Jesse plastered on a fake smile. "Hey. How's it going? I was just leaving."

Luke blocked his path. "I wanted to talk to you."

Jesse looked around and leaned in, lowering his voice. "There's nothing to say. I thought you were...look, I made a mistake. So let's just forget about it and not say anything more."

"Jesse—"

A group of men entered the room, laughing and talking loudly. Jesse used the distraction to bolt for the door, and Luke was about to follow when one of the men slapped him on the back. "Luke Rossovich! Hey, guys, look who it is!"

Luke swore under his breath and let Jesse go, turning to the men with a smile that probably bore more resemblance to a grimace. When he escaped, he looked for Jesse in the clubhouse, but he was long gone.

As he drove home, Luke sped along the freeway until red lights flashed in his rearview. He pulled over with a muttered curse and rolled down his window, waiting for the cop to amble over. "Good afternoon, Officer."

"License and registration." Great, the cop didn't seem to be in the mood for small talk. Luke fished his paperwork out of the glove box and handed it over with his license.

The man looked it over and peered closely at Luke. "You the tennis player?"

Luke smiled sheepishly. "Yeah, that's me. Sorry if I was going too fast. There was a good song on the radio and I guess I just got carried away."

The policeman's mouth curved into a small smile. "You know, I won two hundred dollars on your last Wimbledon title."

"Yeah, I beat the odds on that one." Luke grinned.

"You think I could get an autograph for my wife? She's a big fan."

"Sure! My pleasure. If you give me your address, I'll send her an autographed picture."

The cop scribbled down the info on the back of his pad. "Her name's Nora. I wrote it down for you. Her birthday's coming up; it would be a nice surprise for her."

"No problem, I'll send it off tomorrow."

"Now, you were going about twenty miles over the limit, Mr. Rossovich."

Luke waved his hand. "Please, call me Luke."

"Okay, Luke. I'll let you off with a warning, just this once." The cop winked.

"Thanks, Officer ..." He consulted the paper in his hand. "...Johnston. Much obliged. And I'll be sure to keep to the limit from now on."

"You do that, Luke."

Luke smiled again, nodding goodbye. His celebrity certainly came in handy at times; he couldn't complain. When he arrived home, he went to his office to dig up a glossy headshot to send to Nora Johnston. He made a bad joke about speeding and signed it with a flourish.

As he got up to leave, his eyes wandered over to the bookshelf in the corner. A row of DVDs lined one of the shelves—footage from the best moments in his career. He ran his fingertips across the labels, which were starting to yellow a bit. Night was falling and the living room was almost in darkness. Luke flicked the TV on and played one of the DVDs.

He sank to the floor in front of the couch, looking up at the big TV. Suddenly there he was on court at Wimbledon. It was the second year that he won, when Phillipe Robichaud took him to five sets. He fast-forwarded. The blue light of the TV flickered, casting long shadows across the room.

He watched the final game, which he ended with an ace up the middle at almost a hundred and thirty miles an hour. He sank to the grass onscreen, throwing his hands up in the air. The camera cut to the friend's box, where his mother sat with his coach. Nikolai was standing up, shouting with joy, pumping his fists. He'd been beautiful—tall, ebony-black hair, sculpted muscles. He had a warm smile, a gentleness to him.

Tears sprang to Luke's eyes, unbidden. He watched officials set up for the awards ceremony as he walked around the court, waving to fans. He beckoned for Nik and his mom to come down and met them at the bottom of the stands. He hugged his mother first, and then Nik, slapping his back broadly.

He paused on a shot of them together, smiling as they looked into each other's eyes. Sometimes Luke couldn't believe no one had ever figured it out. He watched their carefree faces, frozen in time.

Later that night, they'd gone back to Luke's hotel room and made love until the early hours of the morning. Luke closed his eyes as he remembered the taste of Nik's mouth, the sensation of

28

being inside him, the two of them lost in their own world.

He turned off the TV before finishing the rest of the recording. Instead, he stayed afloat on his memories.

MIKE DUG OUT a backhand winner that flew just inches past Luke's racquet. "That's another point for me," Mike called out, grinning.

"I thought we weren't keeping score."

"Ha! We're always keeping score, even when we say we aren't." Mike ran a hand over his hair and adjusted the sweatband on his wrist.

Luke served the ball and they smacked it back and forth across the net. Mike was right—Luke always knew exactly how many shots he had missed, how many unforced errors were costing him points that would be valuable in a match. He could calculate his first-serve percentage in his head, didn't need the TV commentators to tell him when it was dropping low.

After he dumped a forehand into the net, Luke stopped to grab some water. "Not my day today."

"Everything okay? You seem distracted."

Luke sighed. He had already heard enough from Aaron; he didn't need Mike chiming in. Not that Mike would be happy about Luke meeting a guy. Aaron was the only one who knew his secret, but he was gay, too. Luke wasn't sure if Mike would be so understanding.

"Sure, everything's fine."

"If you say so."

"I just saw some bit on TV last night about Alex and her new husband. I don't know, I guess I care more than I thought." Luke shrugged. The lies rolled off his tongue easily—had for years.

"Yeah, I understand. Hey, just pretend the ball is him." Mike laughed.

Luke tossed up a ball and served it at well over a hundred miles an hour. "Works like a charm," he said with a grin.

They both laughed and played on. After the rally ended, Mike asked, "Your next tourney is Indian Wells, right? I was thinking of playing Dubai first. Big money prize and all."

"Yeah, but the flight there's pretty pricey." Luke knew Mike wasn't rolling in it, and he hadn't had a great year so far.

"There's the rub. Do I take the chance on winning a bigger prize for my second- or third-round defeat, or just stay home and save money on the flight?"

"You never know, you could win the whole damn thing."

Mike snorted. "Right, like *that's* going to happen."

"Way to think positively. Should I call the sports psychologist?"

"Maybe you should. For you."

"Huh?"

"I said, maybe you should, for you."

Luke tossed a ball sharply into the air, catching it easily in his palm. "I don't need a shrink."

"You've still got what it takes to win the big ones. Your serve is a big bomb, your groundstrokes are as strong as ever, and you're as fit as you were the day you started the tour, save for some wear and tear. But your head's not in it the way it used to be."

"My head's fine. I do everything the shrinks say to do: I picture myself winning; I think positively; I focus on each point as it comes. But sometimes you just don't win. That's the way it goes."

"Maybe you should get a coach again."

"There's nothing a new coach can tell me that I don't already know."

Mike sighed. "Nikolai was a great guy, and a terrific coach. But you never know, someone new could teach you a thing or two."

Luke was flooded with memories and tossed the ball up again as he tried to shake them off. Aaron's words from the beach echoed in his mind. He knew it wouldn't bring Nik back. None of it would—stubbornly refusing to hire a new coach, or pushing away the first person who had dared to get close to him.

He thought of the look on Jesse's face after their kiss. Guilt and longing and anger converged, and Luke felt like screaming. He served a ball instead, smoking it down the center of the court. Mike watched it go by, and then served back his own ball, which they whacked back and forth.

Discussion over.

LUKE MANAGED TO hold out two more days before returning to Brookview. Amber was on the phone and he gave a wave and a wink as he breezed past. He heard her call his name but pretended not to. He wasn't in the mood for flirting. Well, at least not with her.

It wasn't that hard to find the right court, and soon Jesse came into sight, practicing with Jeffrey Sears—a coach who'd been around the block a few times with some champions. Jesse hadn't mentioned anything about him before.

When Jesse noticed Luke watching, he tensed up and his forehand went long. He swore and returned to the baseline, but Jeffrey caught sight of Luke leaning against the outer fence.

"Hey, Rossovich. How's it going?" Jeffrey smiled and nodded his head in greeting. He was getting up there in years, his hair thinning and stomach spreading a bit more every time Luke saw him.

"Jeff." Luke walked towards him and stuck his hand out. "It's going fine. You?"

Jeff pumped his hand and grinned. "Couldn't be better. Got a new pupil, and I'm sure I'll have him whipped into shape in no time."

Jesse shuffled over, stayed a few feet back. "Hey."

"Hey."

"Is there something you needed?" Jesse could barely look him in the eye.

"I just wanted to set up another practice time. You know, for doubles."

Jeff glanced back and forth between them before addressing Jesse. "Doubles? Kid, you never mentioned anything about that."

"It was just an idea, but I don't think it's going to work out." Jesse shrugged.

"Hell, I think it's a great idea! I've only been your coach for two days, but I think it'll do your volleys a world of good."

"So it's settled," Luke said.

"*No.*" Jesse glared at him. "It's not settled. I don't think I have time right now. I need to focus on my own game."

"Look, let's just see how it goes at Indian Wells in a few weeks. One tournament. Besides, this was your idea in the first place," Luke reminded him.

"Hey, Luke, how about you suit up now," Jeff said. "I'll find you two some competition."

"Sure, my stuff's in my car. Gimme ten minutes." Luke could feel Jesse's eyes burning into his back as he left for the parking lot.

Soon, he was back on court and they were facing off against a couple of the club's pros. Despite the fact that he and Jesse barely looked at each other, much less spoke, they won handily. They shook hands with their competitors and Jeff jogged over.

"Nice work, but you two are like singles players out there. If you're going to win against the guys on the tour, you're going to have to play as a *team*. You have to talk out there, come up with signals—you know, *communicate*. You've both been playing alone for too long by the looks of it."

"Yeah, I think you're right," Luke said. Jesse murmured and nodded.

"Okay, let's call it a day, huh?" Jeff slapped Jesse on the back. "Get some rest tonight; I'm working you hard tomorrow! And I'm signing you both up as a doubles team for Indian Wells, so no backing out now."

They headed to the locker room, Jesse speeding ahead. Inside, he quickly opened his locker and shoved his stuff into his gym bag.

"You're not showering?" Luke asked.

"No," he replied, turning to go.

Luke blocked Jesse's path. "Look, I just wanted—"

"To humiliate me?" Jesse lowered his voice, glanced around quickly. They were alone. "I don't know what you're trying to prove, so just leave me alone."

"Jesse, I—"

"Look, I thought you were like me. I was wrong. Now just leave me alone." He tried to brush past, but Luke grabbed his arm.

"I am. Like you."

"What?" Confusion creased Jesse's face. "Bullshit. You couldn't shove me away fast enough."

"Look, you were right. I'm gay," Luke whispered.

"So then…oh. You just…don't like me." Jesse paled. "Right. Okay. I understand." He started to walk away again.

"Oh, for fuck's sake," Luke ground out as he dragged Jesse into the bathroom. He pushed him into a stall and closed the door behind them. For a long moment, they stared at each other, their tense bodies inches apart.

Then Luke grabbed Jesse's head, tangling his fingers in his hair as he pulled him close. Jesse's lips parted beneath his, and Luke slid his tongue inside as they kissed each other, mouths hot and demanding. Jesse clutched him, his fingers digging into Luke's back.

Luke moaned low in his throat. It had been so long. Too long.

When they were both gasping for air, Luke moved to Jesse's neck, the salt of his sweat tangy on Luke's tongue. He slid his hands down to Jesse's ass and squeezed before grinding their growing cocks together.

Luke spun Jesse around and pressed him back against the stall door before he kissed him again, his tongue stroking Jesse's. They rocked their hips together and Luke groaned when Jesse's hands snaked up under his shirt, his fingernails scraping Luke's skin, making him quiver.

Suddenly there was a bark of laughter from the locker room, and they both froze.

"If you think you're going to beat me again next time, you've got another think coming."

"We'll just see about that, pal!" The two men bantered back and forth, for what seemed like forever, until their voices faded into the shower room.

Luke and Jesse were still motionless, their bodies close, chests heaving.

"This is dangerous," Luke muttered.

"Yeah," Jesse agreed.

With effort, Luke stepped backwards, moving as far away as he could in the confines of the stall. "You go out first; I'll wait a minute, just in case."

Jesse nodded. Luke's cock wasn't going to go down anytime soon if he didn't stop looking at Jesse's red, wet lips and the flush in his cheeks. Jesse turned the latch and stepped towards him so the door could swing inwards.

"So, I guess you like me after all, huh?" He grinned and kissed Luke quickly before he was gone.

CHAPTER FIVE

★★★ ★★★

THE PARKING LOT seemed bigger than it was when Luke had parked earlier. Row upon row of cars stretched out in the late afternoon sun as they hurried by.

"My SUV. It's bigger. And the windows are tinted," Luke said. Jesse nodded and they headed towards the vehicle, which still seemed much too far away. When they climbed inside, Jesse didn't waste any time clambering into the back seat. Locking the doors, Luke grinned and joined him.

Luke hadn't made out in a backseat in a very long time, but didn't care as his tongue delved into Jesse's mouth once more. Luke pressed him back against the warm leather, hands roaming his body. The air in the car was hot and stale from being in the sun, and soon they peeled their shirts away from flushed, sweat-slicked skin.

Luke moved down Jesse's body, his knees sliding down to the floor as he yanked Jesse's workout pants down. His firm cock sprang free, and Luke's tongue swirled around the head, teasing the slit. Jesse's hips jerked up and he gasped.

Luke moved further down the shaft, swallowing Jesse into his mouth, sucking him expertly. He pressed Jesse's body down with one hand as the other cupped his balls, rolling them in his palm as his head bobbed up and down. Jesse's fingers clutched at Luke's hair.

Suddenly Jesse was coming, "Oh my god!" escaping his lips as he shot down Luke's throat. Luke swallowed and milked him until Jesse whimpered. Luke wiped his mouth and smiled.

"Sorry. I couldn't last." Jesse flushed and glanced away.

Luke kissed him. "It's okay. I love that you're hot for me."

Jesse traced a small scar on Luke's cheek that had been caused by the corner of the fridge when he had tripped in the kitchen as a boy. "I've been hot for you since the first time I saw you play." Jesse blushed again.

Luke's eyebrow shot up. "Oh, and when was that?"

"When you first won Wimbledon," Jesse mumbled.

"That was nine years ago!"

Jesse smiled. "You were cute, okay?"

"Well, of course I was cute, but you were what, *fourteen?*"

"Oh, and you didn't think guys were hot when you were fourteen?"

"Well, I guess I did." Luke dipped his head and sucked on the soft skin of Jesse's neck. Luke was still hard, and he moved back on top of Jesse, trying to get more pressure on his dick. He licked up the side of Jesse's throat. "Did you fantasize about me?"

Jesse swallowed thickly. "Yes."

"What was I doing?"

"You were fucking me. Hard." Jesse reached down and took hold of Luke's cock, working him as he talked. "I was on my knees and you were so hot and big, and you pounded my ass."

Luke thrust into Jesse's hand as he kissed him, their tongues winding together. "Did I get you off?"

"Always. While you fucked me, you'd jerk my dick like this." Jesse demonstrated on Luke, his hand squeezing tight and moving up and down. "Then you'd hit just the right spot and I'd be gone. Then you'd come inside my ass and fill me up and—"

Luke groaned loudly as he came in long spurts, covering Jesse's hand and splattering their chests. Luke's pulse raced and he took a deep breath, his lips finding Jesse's again, soft and pliant. They lay together for a few minutes before Jesse squirmed.

"I think the door handle is going to be permanently imbedded into my calf."

They laughed and kissed again before cleaning up and getting dressed, elbows and knees bumping from time to time in the confines of the SUV. "You know, you had a pretty vivid imagination for a fourteen-year-old," Luke said.

"Well, I've embellished over the years. Back then, I pretty much just thought of you and it was enough to get me going."

Luke pulled his shirt over his head and chuckled. "You're pretty good for my ego."

"I loved watching you serve. One year when I was just starting college, my whole family watched you at Wimbledon. I had to sit with a cushion on my lap the whole time."

Luke smiled and drew Jesse close for a kiss. "Like I said, good for my ego."

They kissed again before climbing back into the front seat. Jesse pulled a bottle of water from his bag and they passed it back and forth. Luke suddenly couldn't think of anything to say, and for a minute, they said nothing.

"So." Jesse smiled. "I guess I'll see you tomorrow for doubles practice."

"We could practice tonight. At my place." Luke ran his finger up Jesse's thigh, pleased when he saw a shiver run through Jesse's body.

"I can't. I'm having dinner with my parents." He looked at his watch. "Shit, I'm late. I'd better go. But I'll see you tomorrow morning, okay? Your place?"

"Shouldn't we practice here? That way Jeff can give us a hand. You're paying him, after all."

Jesse's face fell just a fraction. "Yeah, sure."

"Or, I guess you could come to my place." Luke leaned over,

his lips hovering near Jesse's ear. "And I could fuck you until you come harder than you ever have before."

Jesse sucked in a breath and his lips found Luke's. When he pulled away, he grinned. "See you bright and early."

Then he was gone, the door slamming shut behind him, as he practically skipped to his car. Luke watched him back out and drive away, finally disappearing around a bend.

Luke stayed where he was, unable to wipe the smile from his face.

A FAMILIAR CAR sat in his driveway when Luke returned home. He pulled up behind it and killed the engine as his mother climbed out of her red Honda Accord, straightening her long jean skirt. Luke had tried many times to buy her a more expensive car, but she'd insisted that she didn't need anything fancy.

"Mom, what are you doing waiting out here?" Luke closed the SUV door behind him and kissed her cheek. "I gave you a key for a reason."

She smiled and hugged him tightly. "I was just passing by and I thought I'd wait a few minutes for you. I don't want to intrude, Luke."

Luke managed to keep a straight face and led her inside. His mother, Stephanie, still lived in Orange County in the house Luke grew up in, and there was no reason for her to be passing by Malibu. Nevertheless, he was happy to see her.

"Can I get you something to drink?"

"Oh, just an iced tea, if you have it."

"One iced tea coming up. Have a seat on the deck, Mom. I'll bring it out."

Luke threw together some snacks on a tray and two glasses of iced tea. His mother was looking out to sea when he joined her outside. He noticed the gray in her shoulder-length hair was a bit more prominent, the silver strands gleaming from amongst the chestnut brown so much like his own. She was sixty now, but Luke didn't think she looked a day over forty-five. He hoped he would age as gracefully.

Stephanie fixed him with a look and a smile, saying nothing. Finally Luke asked, "What?"

"You were whistling."

"I was?" He didn't realize.

"Yes, you were." She took a sip of iced tea. "It's nice to see. You look different, Luke. Happy."

Luke flashed back to the backseat of the SUV, Jesse's cock in his mouth, the taste of his come. He shifted uncomfortably. "Yeah, I guess. Things are good."

"Have you met someone new?"

"Mom, you know how busy I am with the game."

"Too busy for a love life?"

"Mom, gimme a break." Luke forced a laugh. "So, how's the flower shop?"

Stephanie sighed. "There you go."

"There I go what?" Luke had a bad feeling about this. His mother seemed determined to talk about his private life.

"There you go changing the subject. Closing up."

"What? I'm just asking how things are, Mom."

"Business is good. My new apprentice is turning out to be very gifted. I'm quite pleased."

"Glad to hear it."

"Oh, Luke. Don't try to fool me. I'm your mother, remember. It's been a long time since I've seen a spring in your step."

"Mom—"

"Not since Nik died," she said quietly.

Silence settled over them, until Luke finally cleared his throat. "It's been hard. He was a good friend."

She gazed at him closely and took a deep breath. "And a lover."

A buzzing began in Luke's head, getting louder by the second. He stared at his mother, who looked back at him calmly, almost serenely.

He must be dreaming.

Or having a nightmare, to be exact.

"What are you...what you talking about?" Luke's voice sounded strained even to his own ears.

"Did you really think I didn't know? About you and Nik?"

"He was my coach, my friend—"

His mother placed her hand on Luke's arm. "Sweetheart, I've known you were gay for years now. I waited for you to tell me. I decided I was sick of waiting. And that I was sick of seeing you mope around."

Luke said nothing, his heart pounding in his chest, throat dry.

"I know you loved him. But you need to move on. You've only been going through the motions the last few years. I hate to see it. Your father would hate it, too."

He couldn't breathe. "Did he know? Did you tell him?"

Stephanie sighed again. "We never discussed it, but I think he knew. Deep down. He didn't care about that. He loved you, Luke. You know that."

He nodded tersely. His father had died years ago. He'd held on to watch Luke win his first Wimbledon before the cancer took him.

"Luke, you can talk to me. If you've met someone new—"

He stood up abruptly, pushing his chair back. "I haven't."

"But, sweetheart—"

"I have to go. I can't...I just can't." Luke tried to stay calm, but by the time he got past the kitchen, he was running.

He drove aimlessly around the Malibu hills, finally parking up on a lookout, the sun long set. He thought of Nik, closing his eyes and letting himself fall back onto the cushion of his memories.

Nikolai Urmanov had been a few years his senior, a Russian phenom whose career had ended far too soon because of a recurring wrist injury. He'd been living in the States for years, and when he couldn't play the tour anymore, he had decided to stay and coach Luke.

Luke had won his four Grand Slam titles and was number one in the world for almost a year under Nik's tutelage. The media had often remarked warmly upon their close friendship. The Russian who never had a chance to win big, guiding the young American to victory. They were a symbol of the end of the Cold War, a feel-good team that the public adored.

Luke thought of the taste of Nik's lips, the warmth of his skin. He'd had a laugh that boomed out of his chest, and he'd laughed often. Even though his career hadn't been the success he'd wanted, Nik didn't dwell on it; he always looked to the future.

When Luke would get down about his game, Nik would always waggle his finger and say, "*Все дороги ведут в Рим*," which meant, "All roads lead to Rome." Luke would always ask what the hell it was supposed to mean, and Nik would reply, "I don't know, but I think either way, you'll get there in the end." It became a long-standing inside joke, and when Luke won his first Wimbledon, he'd quoted Nik in his victory speech—their own private riddle.

He smiled at the memory, and then felt a flush of shame for what had happened earlier with Jesse. He hadn't been with anyone since Nik's death, had rarely even been tempted. He'd just shut down emotionally, and no one had really caught his attention. Until now.

It had only been two years since Nik, and now Luke was…what? Moving on? Guilt surged through him, and he lunged for the door, barely making it to the ground before vomiting. Tears escaped his eyes after he emptied his stomach, and he gulped in the cool night air.

He couldn't do this. He couldn't just forget Nik. Taking a shaky breath, Luke got back in the SUV. He took a swig of warm water and a moment later realized it was Jesse's bottle from earlier. Guilt tore at him anew and he shuddered.

He returned home hours later to find a note from his mother on the kitchen counter.

Darling,

I made your favorite: macaroni and cheese and chocolate cake for dessert. Please try to eat something. I know this is hard for you, but please remember that all I want is for you to be happy. You can talk to me anytime. I'll always be ready to listen.

Love,
Mom

Luke folded up the letter and tucked it on top of the fridge. His mother knew. He felt like the whole world had just turned on its side, sending him spinning out of control. There was a tightness in his chest, and his stomach churned. She knew, and there was nothing he could do about it.

Nik was still gone. And there was sure as hell nothing Luke could do about that.

It was late, but he reached for the phone. It went to voicemail, and Luke left a message. "Jesse, it's Luke. I think we'd better meet at Brookview tomorrow. Indian Wells is in a week and we could use Jeff's help with training. See you at nine a.m."

It would be better for both of them this way.

CHAPTER SIX

JESSE WAS ALREADY on court with Jeff when Luke arrived. They all said good morning, Jesse shooting Luke an anxious glance. Luke ignored it and suggested they get right to practice.

They played another team from the club, taking a quick lead. When they discussed strategy between points, Luke had a clipped, professional tone to his voice. Jesse mostly just nodded. Jeff shouted instructions from time to time, but overall, they were doing well.

They won the match, and Jeff told them to take five. Luke started working on his serve, willing Jesse to just leave him alone. He saw Jesse approach from the corner of his eye but continued serving.

"So, are you just going to pretend that yesterday didn't happen?" Jesse's voice was tight.

"Look, it was a mistake. I'm sorry, but it can't happen again." Luke threw a ball up and smashed it over the net.

"That's not how it seemed to me. Everything was fine when I left. What happened to change it?"

Luke looked at him, wincing internally when he saw the raw look on Jesse's face. "It's my fault, okay? You didn't do anything wrong. I'm just not ready for this. It's not you."

Jesse barked out a terse laugh. "Oh my god, the first guy I mess around with and I'm already getting the 'It's not you, it's me' speech. That must be some kind of record."

Luke tried to think of something to make Jesse feel better when his words registered. "Wait, what do you mean, 'the first guy'?"

"Nothing, forget it," Jesse mumbled, his cheeks red, eyes downcast.

"Jesse ..." Luke reached out for Jesse's arm, but he backed away.

Jeff chose that moment to jog back onto court. "Okay, ready for a rematch?"

They played on, the tension thick. The other team won easily, 6-3, 6-4. Jeff gave them a lecture on communication afterwards and Luke could barely look him in the eye. This was never going to work; they might as well just give up.

Jesse sped to the locker room. Luke walked quickly to catch up. "Jesse, wait."

He didn't break stride. "Sorry, I'm in a rush."

Luke caught him by the elbow and tugged him into an alcove. "Look, maybe we should just cancel out on Indian Wells."

Jesse squared his jaw. "Why? You afraid?"

"No! What the hell would I have to be afraid of?"

Jesse shook his head and shrugged. "I don't know, Luke. You tell me." When Luke said nothing, Jesse sighed. "Jeff already committed us. We'll get a penalty if we withdraw without a good reason. If you want to quit, then you go tell Jeff right now. I don't want to hear the lecture. I don't deserve it." With that, he walked off.

Luke paced the hallway a bit before he found Jesse in the locker room. He tried not to notice the way Jesse's firm muscles flexed in his back as he pulled a shirt over his head. Luke cleared his throat. "Okay, we'll play."

Jesse looked over his shoulder and nodded. "Okay." He closed his locker and picked up his bag. "It's business, plain and simple."

Luke knew it was anything but.

THE DAY OF Luke and Jesse's first match at Indian Wells dawned cool, but soon warmed up as the sun rose. Luke and Mike hit a practice court and rallied for a few hours. They were both into the second round of singles, as was Jesse. Luke hadn't seen him yet but had watched the highlights on TV in his hotel room.

Their last few practice sessions together had been torture, but they were playing well enough as a team. Jesse had become just as cold and clinical as Luke was, and Luke wondered again why they didn't just pay the penalty for withdrawal. But here they were, scheduled for one of the outer courts against a French/South African team.

Luke met Jesse in the locker room before the match. He put down his equipment and started stretching. Jesse had only nodded at him when he'd walked in, so finally Luke asked, "How's it going?"

Jesse looked up from tightening the strings on his racquet. "Fine." He looked back down, staring intently at nothing.

Luke couldn't think of anything else to say, so he continued stretching his hamstring. The silence between them was heavy, and Luke was relieved when their opponents arrived. They made small talk until called out onto the court.

Jesse and Luke won the coin toss and chose to serve first. Luke's first serve was an ace, neither of the other players managing to get their racquets on it. They won the first game easily, and before Luke knew it, he and Jesse had taken the first set.

On the changeover, when players switched sides of the court, he and Jesse sat in their chairs on the sideline and drank some water.

"I think we should go more to Morel's backhand; it's looking pretty shaky," Jesse said.

"Yeah, sounds like a plan."

Jesse swallowed another gulp of water as the official called time and nodded. He trotted out past the net, Luke trailing behind him. They took the lead in the second set and things were running smoothly until a ball that Luke let sail by him was called in, not out as he'd expected. Now they were down break point. He was sure the ball hadn't touched the line and approached the chair umpire.

"Come on, that ball was out by a mile."

The umpire remained impassive. "The linesman made the right call. It looked like it clipped the line. I'm not overruling."

Luke looked up into the ump's face, his calm, emotionless features. Suddenly he felt something inside him give way. "Bullshit!" he yelled.

The ump's jaw tightened. "Return to your position on the court and resume play."

"Or what?" Luke sneered. Then he felt a tug on his arm and Jesse was there.

"Shut up and play." Jesse glared, teeth clenched.

Luke finally nodded, going back to the baseline. They continued on, and after a close call on one of Luke's service games, continued to pull ahead. On match point, Morel's forehand flew long. Neither Jesse nor Luke showed much emotion, just high-fived each other for show. Still, Luke couldn't help but feel a jolt when their palms touched.

They shook hands with their opponents and returned to their chairs to collect their gear. Jesse was stone-faced, and Luke couldn't blame him. By their lockers, Luke cleared his throat after glancing around to make sure no one was in hearing range. "Sorry. About today. Out there. It won't happen again."

Jesse slammed his locker. "You're damn right it won't. You can throw tantrums when it's just you out there, but I don't play like that."

"I know. I'm sorry, okay?"

"Yeah, fine. I've got to go practice for my match tomorrow." He stalked out, bag slung over this shoulder. Luke retreated to the shower room, but all the hot water in the world couldn't release the tension coiled in his muscles.

"GEEZ, WHAT DID that cow ever do to you?"

Luke looked up from his plate, where he was tearing into his New York strip steak.

"Huh?"

Mike nodded towards Luke's plate. "Got a little pent-up frustration?"

Luke realized he was gripping his steak knife so hard his knuckles were white. He forced a laugh and took a deep breath. "Yeah, it's been a long day."

"You won your doubles though, right? Hell, I never thought I'd see the day when Luke Rossovich played doubles on tour again."

"Yeah, I didn't think I'd see it, either." Luke concentrated on his food.

"What's the kid like?"

Luke shrugged, hoping he looked casual. "Nice enough. He's quick on his feet. Good player."

Mike smiled. "Great. Hey, you never know, you guys could make a great couple."

"What?" Luke choked on his beer, and it dribbled down his chin.

"You know, like McEnroe and Fleming. Although you're a bit long in the tooth to be starting a doubles dynasty now. But hey, you never know, right?"

"Right." Luke smiled. He took a mouthful of green beans, since he couldn't think of anything else to say. He swallowed and asked, "How's Shelley like the new dishwasher?"

"Loves it. She'd better; it took me hours to install."

"You know, you can pay people to do that," Luke joked.

"Well, we all don't have big Top Spin contracts on account of our pretty faces, now do we? Some of us have to work for a living!" Mike grinned.

They traded barbs back and forth, and for a while Luke didn't feel quite so weighed down.

LUKE LOST IN his next singles match, and then had to be on court to play with Jesse an hour later. Despite the fact that they only spoke when necessary, they managed to pull out a win. Luke had half a mind to just tank the match so he wouldn't have to play with Jesse again, but the competitor in him wouldn't allow it.

The locker room was packed, and he and Jesse chatted with some of the guys, which spared them having to talk to each other. Luke made a quick escape, but ran into Stein Koehler, the world's current number one. The German was tall, dark and very, very handsome. Also very, very straight. Not to mention an asshole.

"Luke," Koehler drawled. "Tough loss today."

Luke squared his shoulders and smiled coldly. "Well, you know how it goes. Win some, lose some."

"But you did win your *doubles* match, no?" Koehler infused the word with all the contempt he could muster.

"Yep."

"Well, at least that's something to be proud of."

Luke smiled tightly and nodded, saying "Later," before he kept walking down the hall. A car was waiting to whisk him back to his hotel. He dumped his stuff in his room and had a long, hot shower.

Soon, he found himself down at the hotel bar. The bartender, a cute woman with curly red hair and a big smile, flirted with him. He flirted back, and her pours became longer and longer.

"So, I get off in ten minutes," she said, voice husky. "And you can, too."

Luke swallowed the rest of his drink, the ice rattling in his glass. He smiled and shook his head. "Sorry. I need my beauty sleep."

"Oh, playing hard to get, huh?" She licked her lips and leaned over the bar, showing off her impressive breasts.

Luke fished out his wallet and plunked down more than enough for the bill and a generous tip. "Like I said, sorry." He spun around on his stool and walked away, the bartender pouting in his wake.

Luke wasn't that drunk, but as the elevator door closed, he leaned back, eyes drifting shut. The doors opened a second later, and he opened his eyes to find Jesse with one foot on the elevator, the other still in the lobby.

They stared at each other until the door started moving shut again. Jesse hurried inside and jabbed the button for his floor. As the elevator ascended, Luke cleared his throat.

"Luke." Jesse's voice was sharp. "Just don't say anything, okay? I get it. You don't like me. End of story."

"Then how come I can't stop thinking about you?" The truth slipped off his tongue, loosened by too much whiskey. Luke cursed himself.

Jesse looked at him as if Luke had two heads. "Is this some kind of game? Do you enjoy this?" His voice rose, nostrils flaring. "I don't find it amusing, okay? You've humiliated me enough, thanks."

"It's not a game."

The elevator stopped, the doors sliding open. It was Jesse's floor, and for a moment, he remained immobile, their eyes locked. In that moment, Luke knew. He knew that he wanted Jesse McAllister.

For the first time in two years, Luke really felt alive.

Luke pulled Jesse to him, the doors closing once more. As Jesse gasped in surprise, Luke kissed him, slipping his tongue inside his mouth. Jesse was stiff and unyielding, his hands pushing against Luke's chest. Luke could feel Jesse's dick start to harden, and he slid his hands down to Jesse's ass, pulling him closer.

With a soft moan, Jesse gave in, his arms wrapping around Luke, their tongues twisting together. They rubbed against each other as they kissed, teeth clashing, lips wet. Soon they were panting for breath, and Luke's hands were still gripping Jesse's firm ass.

The elevator doors opened with a ping.

It took them a few seconds to realize what was happening and they leapt apart, dazed. Panic blazed through Luke's gut, and he expected to see paparazzi, or the chesty bartender, or maybe Stein Koehler and his sneer.

No one peered back. They had arrived at Luke's floor, the penthouse.

"Jesus," Luke muttered. The doors began closing, and Luke reached out a hand to stop them. With his other, he tugged Jesse. Jesse didn't move, and Luke looked back. "Come on."

Jesse shook his head. "Not if this is all going to be a mistake tomorrow."

Luke took a deep breath and threaded their fingers together. "No more games."

"Promise?"

"Promise." Luke felt like he was spinning again, out of control.

This time, he didn't want it to stop.

CHAPTER SEVEN

THEY STUMBLED INTO Luke's suite, the door closing firmly behind them. They kissed and tugged at each other's clothing as they made their way through the living room and into the bedroom.

Luke pressed Jesse back onto the bed in the dark room, pinning him down. He pulled Jesse's shirt off and moved his lips over his nipples, going back and forth between them as he yanked at Jesse's pants. Jesse's cock strained against his white cotton briefs, and Luke's head dipped low, his mouth moving over the cotton.

Jesse moaned, his fingers twisting in Luke's hair. He pulled Luke back up, his tongue diving into Luke's mouth as his hips arched up. Luke broke away and yanked his own clothes off before he straddled Jesse, naked. Luke stroked his own dick, and Jesse's eyes widened with desire, his pink tongue darting out to lick his lips.

Luke pulled Jesse's cock out of his briefs and held it to his, rubbing both of them together tightly. Jesse thrust upwards and groaned as Luke picked up the pace, his fingers digging into Luke's thighs. Luke stroked their slick cocks together, his hips thrusting in time with his hand as they got closer and closer to the edge.

Jesse's head was thrown back, his mouth open as he began to shudder, his come hitting his chest. Luke's balls tightened at the sight, and soon he was shooting hard, spilling over his hand.

He rolled off Jesse and they lay on the bed side by side, the light from the moon shining through the big window. As Luke's pulse began to return to normal, he shifted closer, his tongue finding the come drying on Jesse's chest. He licked it up, the flavor making need unfurl in his belly once more. Jesse watched him with big eyes.

"Roll over," Luke whispered.

Suddenly Jesse tensed up. "Luke, I ..."

"It's okay, I know." He rubbed his hand soothingly down Jesse's stomach. "I just want to taste you."

Jesse's brow creased. "But...you just did."

Luke grinned and gently pushed on Jesse's shoulder until he rolled over. He slowly dragged Jesse's underwear down his legs, lips following close behind. Then he kissed his way back up, nudging Jesse's legs open with his head. He could hear shallow breathing above him, and when his tongue flicked across Jesse's hole, Jesse gasped.

Luke kissed and licked Jesse's hole, working his pointed tongue inside as Jesse began to writhe against the mattress, moans of pleasure escaping his lips. Luke drove him to the edge, his spit dripping down Jesse's shaking thighs. Luke urged him up onto his knees, and with a few tugs on his cock, Jesse came again, Luke's tongue still buried in his ass.

Jesse collapsed, and Luke turned him over onto his back. Jesse's mouth was slack, and Luke straddled his body once more, bringing his cock to Jesse's lips. Jesse's tongue snaked out, his mouth covering the head, lips sucking firmly. Luke was hard as a rock and he wanted to fuck Jesse's mouth, wanted to shove his cock deep into Jesse's throat.

Instead he pulled back, his own hand quickly pumping his shaft. It was possible Jesse had never sucked anyone off and Luke didn't want to go too far, too fast. He brought himself off quickly, head back, thighs gripping Jesse's body beneath him. He rolled off onto his side to catch his breath, his legs entangled with Jesse's.

"So," Jesse said a few minutes later, "that's what rimming feels like."

"Yeah. Like it?"

Jesse's head turned towards him. "Hell, yes." He grinned.

Luke ran his fingers up Jesse's chest idly. "So you...don't have much experience?"

"I know, it's lame."

"It's not lame." Luke drew Jesse's face back towards him, his finger under his chin. "It's hot, actually." He kissed him softly.

"It is?" Jesse smiled shyly.

"It is." Just the thought of being the first one inside Jesse's ass, how tight he would be—Luke felt a heady rush of desire. "So how did a guy as gorgeous as you not get fucked ten ways to Sunday by the time you were sixteen?"

Jesse took a deep breath and blew it out. "Something happened when I was younger. Did a real number on me, I guess."

"What happened?" Luke felt a sick feeling in the pit of his stomach. "I mean, if you want to tell me."

Jesse took a deep breath and blew it out slowly. "There was this guy who lived next door. Rich Sadler, his name was. We used to play together, and when we were around twelve, stuff started to happen. We messed around, jerked each other off. One day in his garage, I kissed him." Jesse shook his head, lost in the memory. "He freaked out, starting punching me. I ran home and locked myself in the bathroom for hours; told my mom later that I'd gotten in a fight over a comic book."

Luke brushed the hair from Jesse's forehead. "I'm sorry." He hated the thought of someone hurting Jesse.

"It gets better. A few days later, Rich comes over and tells me he's sorry. Wants to make it up to me." Jesse grimaced. "I was so stupid, so trusting. I went with him to the woods where we had a tree house. Some other guys from the neighborhood were waiting. I ran, but they caught me. Called me faggot, kicked me, spit on me. The grand finale was when they pissed all over me."

"Bastards." Luke tried to control the anger surging up inside him. He felt like breaking something, preferably someone's face. He pulled Jesse closer, pillowing Jesse's head on his chest as he rubbed his back.

"After that, I started putting all my effort into tennis, into running. I told myself that I may be a faggot, but no one was ever going to catch me again." Jesse sniffed. "I bet you're sorry you asked, huh? God, I'm not normally this melodramatic, I swear."

Luke kissed the top of Jesse's head. "I'm not sorry. Only for the way I've been acting. I've got my own issues, as I'm sure you've noticed."

"Uh, yeah. You could say that."

Luke thought about telling Jesse about Nik, but the words died on his tongue. Somehow, it felt wrong to talk about him with Jesse warm and alive in his arms.

Jesse laughed with a hint of nervousness. "Well, we're quite a pair. We could keep a shrink busy for hours on end. Our neuroses have neuroses."

Luke found himself chuckling, too, much to his surprise. "You can say that again."

The smile left Jesse's face and he looked intently at Luke. "So...where does that leave us?" He ducked his head. "I really like you. A lot." His eyes found Luke's again. "But if you're not ready for this, tell me now."

Luke took a deep breath, blowing it out slowly. Was he ready? Could he let someone else in, let Jesse get close? Jesse bit his lip, watching him anxiously. Luke thought about how his life had been before Nik died. Thought about the emptiness after.

His lips met Jesse's, his hand cupping his face. "I'm ready."

They kissed slowly, with no fire, no rush. Jesse turned on his side and Luke spooned up close behind him, Jesse's hair soft on Luke's cheek. As he drifted away, Luke dreamt of running over a huge green tennis court, the grass soft beneath his feet.

WHEN LUKE WOKE the next morning, he was alone. He shook off the stupor of sleep and sat up in bed, his heart rate increasing.

He really, really wanted Jesse to still be there.

The faint sound of running water reached his ears and he noticed the bathroom door was closed. Relief coursed through him as he nudged the door open and saw Jesse's form through the opaque shower curtain.

"Hey." Jesse blinked water out of his eyes as Luke pulled back the curtain. "Sorry, I didn't want to wake you."

Luke stepped in and closed the curtain behind him. "You didn't." He pulled Jesse close for a kiss. His morning hard-on wasn't going anywhere as his hands roamed over Jesse's slick, soapy skin.

Jesse purred appreciatively as he rubbed up against Luke. "Maybe I should have." He found a sensitive spot on Luke's neck, sucking until Luke moaned. Jesse's mouth moved down Luke's body until he was on his knees. Luke ran his fingers through Jesse's silky hair.

"It's okay, you don't have to."

"I want to." Jesse was already breathing hard in anticipation.

Luke wavered on his feet as Jesse took him into his hot mouth. One hand moved around the shaft, the other gripping Luke's hip as he licked and sucked. For what he lacked in experience, he more than made up for in enthusiasm, and the sight of Jesse on his knees, Luke's cock in his mouth, made Luke's balls tighten quickly.

After another minute he panted, "Watch out," trying to move

Jesse's head away. But Jesse didn't move, sucking harder as he held Luke to him. Luke groaned as he came, Jesse swallowing and coughing a bit before Luke hauled him up to his feet, smiling.

Jesse licked his lips, satisfied. "You taste pretty good."

Luke leaned down and kissed him thoroughly. "Yeah, I do," he said, swatting him on the ass.

They both giggled, and Jesse tried to slap Luke's ass right back, but Luke twisted away. It turned into a wrestling match that ended with a torn shower curtain and water splashed all over the bathroom floor.

Luke couldn't remember when he'd laughed so much.

"YOU KNOW, I don't think I've ever seen Luke Rossovich playing doubles," Steve Anderson remarked to his partner in the booth. "Most of the top players can't be bothered these days and prefer to focus on their singles matches."

Luke served an ace up the middle and slapped hands with Jesse. They were down a set and a break, but still playing well.

"I don't think Rossovich and McAllister are going to be able to beat the Stifflers today; the Aussie brothers are the number-one doubles team in the world for a reason. Still, it's nice to see two American singles players teaming up and making it into the doubles finals here at Indian Wells. And Jesse made it to the quarters against Jean-Paul Riel, so he's playing pretty well of late."

A rally of volleys took place at the net, with Jesse finally getting one past the brothers. "Nice one!" Steve exclaimed. "Rossovich and McAllister looked a bit shaky early on in the tournament, but now they're talking to each other a lot more on court and that seems to have made a difference. It'll be interesting to see how they play in Miami in a couple of weeks; I hear they've entered as a doubles team again."

On match point, Jesse's backhand dive went long. He and Luke clasped hands briefly before going to congratulate their opponents. As they left the court, they stopped to sign autographs. "Ross has always been very popular with the fans," Steve remarked. "And it's good exposure for Jesse McAllister—after all, we probably wouldn't have broadcast this match if one of America's favorite players wasn't involved. It's great for tennis."

Even though the cameras were focused on Luke and Jesse, Steve put on a cheesy grin as he said, "Let's hope this is the start of a beautiful partnership."

CHAPTER EIGHT

★★★ ★★★

THE SKY WAS a deep blue, the midday sun making the blacktop shimmer as Luke and Jesse drove back towards the coast through the California desert. The top was down on Luke's Porsche and iced cappuccino slid easily down his throat.

Life was good.

"So what did you tell Jeff about coming with me?"

"Just told him we wanted to talk strategy for our next competition." Jesse's hand drifted over to Luke's thigh. "Didn't mention how I wanted to suck your dick again on the way back."

Laughing, Luke said, "Yeah, then I crash the car and the police catch me with my pants down. We'll just have to wait until we get home." Home. For once, Luke actually looked forward to going back there. No one had been in his bedroom since Nik, and it was time.

Jesse's cell rang, and he answered. "Hello? Oh, hey, Mom." He looked over at Luke and smiled nervously. "Oh, right. No, of course I remembered. I'll be there. Okay. Hmm? No, I'm riding back with Luke. You know, Luke Rossovich. Yeah, he's nice, Mom."

Luke grinned devilishly and reached over to stroke Jesse through his jeans. Jesse bit back a gasp. "What? Oh, it was nothing, I just spilled my drink. Okay, talk to you later." He hung up and smacked Luke's arm. "I thought you didn't want to get into an accident?"

Luke shrugged. "Changed my mind. Not that much traffic out here in the desert."

"Just keep your eyes on the road," Jesse said with a laugh.

"Fine, fine." Luke smiled. "So what did your mom want?"

Jesse groaned. "I totally forgot about my parents' anniversary party tonight. There's no way I can get out of it."

Luke felt a flare of disappointment. "It's okay, I understand."

"You know I'd rather be with you, right? But they're my parents, so ..."

"I know. I understand, really." Luke smiled reassuringly.

"I'll see you tomorrow though?"

"You'd better. I've quickly become accustomed to getting off multiple times a day."

Jesse laughed. "You mean you didn't before? Your hand muscles are in pretty good condition."

"No, no, you're the one who jerked off all the time thinking of me, remember?"

"Yeah, I remember." Jesse's voice lowered, a wistful look coming over his face. "Sometimes I feel like I'm dreaming, you know? Like any second I'll wake up and I'll be alone and you'll still be a stranger I watch on TV sometimes, or see glimpses of at tournaments."

Luke reached over and took Jesse's hand. "I'm not going anywhere."

"Good to know." Jesse leaned over and kissed him quickly.

They drove on in comfortable silence for a while, the wind whipping by. "So, your parents," Luke said. "Do they know? That you're gay?"

"No. Sometimes I think they must suspect. I mean, I've never had a girlfriend. Although in college, I just told them I was too busy with school and tennis. Which was true. I just didn't bring up how I like guys."

"Wouldn't go down too well?"

Jesse shrugged. "I honestly don't know. They're liberal, I guess, but...I just wonder how they'd react. My father's only son turning out to be queer. I don't think he'd be too thrilled. Maybe I'm afraid to find out."

"Yeah, I understand."

"Does your mom know? Your dad died a long time ago, right?"

Luke nodded, his chest tightening. It didn't seem to matter how much time passed; it still hurt to think of him. His dad missed out on so much. "Nine years. I guess it's a long time."

"Sorry, I didn't mean to sound dismissive or anything."

"It's okay. You didn't."

"So, did he know?"

"No. But apparently my mother wasn't so easily fooled."

"You never told her yourself?"

"I just never got around to it, I guess. Never seemed like the right time."

Silence stretched out until Jesse said, "How do you know? That she knows?"

"She told me. Last week. Seems that she knew about me and...and she was wondering if I had a new boyfriend."

"Oh. Um, so what did you say?" Jesse shifted in his seat, uncomfortable.

"I didn't say much. I ran away. From her. From you."

"Oh. That's why ..."

"Yeah. It was a bit too much to take in all at once. I'm sorry." Luke cleared his throat. It felt strange to say it all out loud.

"It's okay, I get it." Jesse smiled and his hand found Luke's thigh again. He didn't squeeze or make any sexual advances, just rested it there until they were back in LA, the noise and the smog enveloping them.

AFTER DROPPING JESSE off with a long kiss and a promise to meet the next day, Luke found himself heading towards his mother's house. It was the same small house he'd grown up in, with the well-kept lawn, neat flowerbeds, and big oak tree in the backyard.

When Stephanie opened the door, she smiled. "You still have a key, you know."

"I know," Luke said, sheepish. "I just thought maybe …"

"Oh, Luke." She drew him into her arms tightly. "You never have to knock."

He breathed her in—the familiar scent of the same perfume she'd worn his whole life, the freshly laundered smell of her button-down shirt. "I'm sorry, Mom."

She pulled back and shut the door behind him, leading him to the couch. "For what, sweetheart?"

Luke shrugged. "For everything. For lying to you and Dad. For being…who I am."

"I love you, Luke. Just the way you are. I always have." She kissed his cheek gently. "Don't forget that."

He felt like a weight had left his shoulders. "I love you, too, Mom."

"I know." She tucked a strand of hair behind her ear and fiddled briefly with the simple pearl earring she wore. "Luke, just promise me something."

"What?"

"That you'll be honest with me. All these years I've waited for you to say something. Did you think I wouldn't understand?"

Guilt coursed through him. "Mom, it wasn't your fault. You've always been there for me." He took her hand. "I couldn't have asked for a better mother. I guess I was just scared."

"Did you really think I'd turn my back on you?"

"I…I don't know. It's just…people have these expectations of me and I'm afraid that if they find out the truth nothing will be the same."

"People can surprise you, dear." She squeezed his fingers.

"Yeah, they can." He sighed. "I wanted to tell you, but I had to keep Nik a secret. I would never have gotten those endorsements otherwise. No matter how many Grand Slams I won."

"Yes, I suppose you're right."

"And then he died, and...I don't know. It was too hard. I didn't want to talk about it with anyone. I just wanted to forget it."

"I know. He was a wonderful man. I always liked him."

"Yeah," he said, swallowing the lump in his throat.

"But you can't keep living in the past, Luke."

"I'm not, Mom."

"Honey, I know what it's like to lose the person you love. After your father died, I felt like I was sleepwalking for so long. Just ..."

"Going through the motions," Luke finished.

"But eventually it's okay for things to be normal. To be happy again."

"I think maybe I'm just starting to believe that."

Stephanie hugged him again, rubbing his back soothingly, the way she did when he was a child with a nightmare. Luke knew she was fighting tears, and he blinked rapidly himself. When she sat back, she said, "Well, why don't you tell me about this young man you've met."

Luke huffed out a nervous laugh. "What?"

"You know who I'm talking about."

"Mom ..."

"The one who inspired you to actually play *doubles* on the tour. Jesse McAllister, I believe his name is." She smiled knowingly.

"How did you...was it that obvious? On TV?" Panic stabbed

Luke's gut.

"No, no, don't worry. But I'm your mother, dear. You can't fool me," she said, winking.

Luke smiled and found himself telling her everything, the words flowing so easily he wondered why he'd waited so long.

Later as she cooked dinner, Luke wandered up to his old room. The door stood open and for a few moments he stood on the threshold, as if he was entering some kind of shrine. His childhood trophies and awards still gleamed from the bookshelf, and his bedspread was the racing car motif he'd begged for at the age of fifteen.

He tentatively sat on the bed, as if it would collapse underneath his adult weight. It held firm and Luke bounced up and down a bit, the springs creaking just slightly. The ink stain on the carpet by his desk remained, a reminder of the ballpoint pen that had leaked all over his English homework one night. The pen had been a gift from his grandfather, and Luke had kept it, even though it was useless.

He crossed to the desk and opened the top drawer, the shell of the pen still there where he'd left it. His Transformers eraser set also rested in the drawer, untouched by lead. It had been one of his earliest prized possessions.

Movement outside the window captured his attention and Luke moved back to his bed to peer out. A bird fluttered on the tree outside before flying away. Luke rested his chin on the windowsill and looked at his street, all the houses achingly familiar. It was a view he could close his eyes and still see perfectly, no matter where in the world he was. He'd spent countless nights at the window, dreaming of the future.

"Luke! Dinner." Stephanie's voice floated up the stairs, and for a moment the déjà vu was almost too much.

Shaking himself, Luke got up and headed out of his room, shutting the drawer in the old desk as he passed.

IT WAS LATE when the doorbell rang, the chimes echoing through the house. Luke padded downstairs and peered out the window beside the front door. He quickly opened up.

"Jesse. Is everything okay?"

Jesse smiled up at him slyly. "It's tomorrow."

Desire sprang to life instantly, and Luke laughed as he pulled Jesse in by his shirt, pressing him up against the door when he closed it. "Just couldn't wait, huh?" Luke asked between kisses, his hands moving over Jesse's lithe body.

Jesse moaned and stroked Luke's tongue with his own, hands twisting in Luke's T-shirt. "I want you to fuck me," he rasped. "I *need* you to fuck me. Please."

Luke sure as hell didn't need to be asked twice, and propelled Jesse up the stairs. They got stuck halfway up, limbs tangled, lips bruising with the force of their kisses, their hunger.

Luke broke away, panting. "Come on, I want you in my bed." He wasn't about to deflower Jesse on the hard wooden stairs.

They made their way to his room, quickly shedding their clothes. Luke covered Jesse's body with his own on the mattress, his mouth and hands roaming. They were both hard as rock, and Jesse bucked his hips anxiously. Licking along Jesse's stomach, up over his chest, Luke flicked his nipples as he went by. When he caught Jesse's earlobe between his teeth, Luke practically growled, "You want me to fuck you?"

"Yes, oh god, yes!"

Luke slipped his index finger into Jesse's mouth, Jesse's tongue eagerly swirling around it. When it was slick with saliva, Luke reached down and gently slipped it inside. He pushed in slowly, past the ring of muscle and into the waiting heat. Jesse's eyes went wide, and his legs opened further. Luke chuckled. "Well, aren't you the wanton one?"

Slithering down on the mattress, Luke held Jesse's ass up so his tongue could follow his finger's path. He licked and sucked at Jesse's hole until Jesse was writhing above him in anticipation.

Luke leaned over the side of the bed and opened the drawer on the bedside table. He found the lube first, then pulled out a plastic package, breathing a sigh of relief that the condoms weren't expired. While he tore open one of the wrappers, Jesse moved onto his hands and knees.

Running his hand through Jesse's hair, Luke said, "Not the first time," and urged him back over. Jesse's cheeks flushed even more than they already were, and he laughed nervously.

"There's lots of different ways," Luke whispered. He leaned down and kissed him as he moved between Jesse's legs, placing them up on his shoulders.

Jesse nodded and Luke's lips found his again as he slipped the condom on. The lube was cold, and he warmed it in his palm while he kissed Jesse, trying to relax him. He spread the lube on his dick and rubbed it into Jesse's hole.

"Ready?"

Taking a deep breath, Jesse smiled. "Yes."

Luke went slowly, pushing into him inch by inch. Jesse's eyes rounded and he gripped Luke's arm. "Oh, my god," he gasped. "It hurts."

"I know. It's okay," Luke stroked Jesse's cock lightly with one hand to distract him as he moved deeper inside. When he was in almost all the way, he stopped and let Jesse get accustomed to the feeling. Jesse's knees pressed into his chest, and Luke grinned. "It's a good thing you're so flexible."

Jesse laughed shakily, and Luke could feel him relax enough for him to pull out a bit and drive back in a bit harder. They both moaned loudly, and when Luke established a rhythm of shallow thrusts, Jesse's mouth opened, his eyes closing in a mixture of pleasure and pain.

"Oh god, oh god," Jesse murmured. Luke moved in deeper and bent to kiss him, his tongue plunging into Jesse's mouth in tandem with Luke's cock in his ass. Jesse was rock hard between them, and he whimpered when Luke shifted back without touching him.

Jesse opened his eyes and looked up at Luke with a sense of wonder. A smile danced over his lips as he reached up, his fingers on Luke's cheek as their bodies strained together.

"God, you're fucking beautiful," Luke muttered.

Jesse's smile grew. "That's what I was about to say."

They kissed again, and Luke moaned. Jesse was so hot and tight, and Luke knew he wouldn't last much longer. Sweat dripped down the hollow of his back and his muscles shook as he fought to stay in control. He wanted Jesse to come first, and he reached for his cock between them, stroking it roughly.

Jesse threw his head back as he came, mouth open, body shuddering. Luke thrust once more and followed, moaning as his body shook with waves of pleasure. He collapsed, Jesse's legs sliding off his shoulders. They stayed there for a minute, Jesse's heart pounding beneath Luke's ear.

After Luke eased out and disposed of the condom, he brought back a washcloth and wiped Jesse's chest clean. Pulling him into his arms, they rested, heads together on the pillow, Jesse's breath warm on Luke's neck.

"I can't believe I just had sex with Luke Rossovich."

"I know, I'm pretty fucking amazing, huh?"

Jesse slapped Luke's chest with his palm, giggling. "Glad to see you've still got that healthy ego."

"Yeah, well. You're pretty fucking amazing, too." He pressed their lips together. "Really amazing," he murmured.

When he woke just after dawn, Luke didn't move, just listened to Jesse snore softly as sunlight crept in through the windows.

CHAPTER NINE

"COME ON, OLD man, try to keep up!" Jesse sprinted ahead, sand flying in his wake.

Luke grimaced as he willed an extra burst of speed into his legs. His lungs burned, having already run out to the cove and almost all the way back. They were on the stretch of beach in front of his house when he managed to catch up to Jesse. He yanked Jesse's shirt, and soon they were in the sand, rolling around, wrestling for dominance.

"So, I guess you've already had a run today," a voice said.

Luke and Jesse sprung apart and squinted up at Aaron, who was sauntering over, an amused expression on his face. "I guess you forgot I was coming, Luke." He grinned.

Luke sighed in defeat. "Aaron Slater, meet Jesse McAllister."

"Hey, Jesse. Nice to meet you." Aaron offered Jesse a hand up from the sand.

"Nice to meet you, too. You're Luke's trainer?" Jesse brushed sand from his body and smiled nervously.

"Yep. And you're …"

"His doubles partner," Jesse quickly said.

"Ahhhh. Right. I'm sure you're having a great time playing *doubles.*" Aaron winked at Luke.

"Yeah, we are. We were in the finals at Indian Wells, and we're playing next week in Miami. Then clay-court season starts, and I guess we'll see how it goes." Jesse's words tumbled out.

Luke stood up and brushed himself off. "It's okay, Jesse. I'm afraid Aaron is on to us."

Jesse looked back and forth between them. "He is?"

"Sorry, honey, no pulling the wool over this queer's eyes." Aaron laughed.

"Oh." Jesse's face flushed.

"Well, Luke, are you ready for your workout? Unless the kid's already tired you out." Aaron winked at Jesse, whose blush deepened.

"I'll meet you in the gym."

Aaron nodded and waved to Jesse before jogging up the steps to the house.

"So, has he always known?"

"Yeah. Took him about five seconds to figure it out, to hear him tell it. I'm not convinced; I think I fooled him for a good half hour."

Jesse smiled. "I guess our secret is safe with him?"

"Yeah, I trust him. Don't worry." Luke glanced around at the deserted beach before quickly pecking Jesse's lips. "I'd better go. Think you can keep yourself busy for a couple of hours?"

"Don't worry about me. I've got to practice my serve or Jeff will kick my ass this afternoon."

Aaron was waiting in Luke's home gym, which featured ceiling-to-floor plate glass windows and a killer view of the ocean. "So, he's the new guy, huh?"

Luke lay down on the bench press and waited for Aaron to load up the barbell. "Yeah, that's him."

"Cute as hell. And nice ass."

Luke started his chest presses, heaving the weight up and down while Aaron hovered overhead. "You have no idea."

"Seems sweet, too."

"Yeah. He's ..." Luke grunted as he lifted the weight up, his muscles fatiguing. Aaron took the barbell and put it back in its holder. "Great," Luke continued as he sat up.

"It's nice to see you like this, Luke."

"Like what?"

Aaron handed him a dumbbell and Luke dutifully started his bicep curls. "Happy. Relaxed. You've had a tough couple of years, and you deserve some happiness."

"Yeah, I guess so."

Aaron wandered over to the window. "You know, I could use some happiness myself these days, so if you get sick of him ..." Luke threw him a look and Aaron raised his hands. "Okay, just kidding."

As he stretched his arms, Luke joined Aaron at the window. Jesse was down below on the court, a basket of balls beside him at the baseline. He served one ball after another until they were all gone and then collected them from the other side of the court. Luke watched him until Aaron cleared his throat pointedly.

"Hmm?" Luke glanced at him.

Aaron laughed and looked at his watch. "Three minutes, twenty-three seconds."

"What?"

"And if I hadn't interrupted you, you'd still be staring at him."

Luke shook his head and stalked over to the leg press. "You know, I don't pay you for commentary."

"Then I am *really* undercharging."

They laughed, and Luke went to work on his legs while Aaron counted out the repetitions and urged him to keep going when he got tired. When Aaron started telling him about a new low-carb diet, Luke's mind drifted back to the court below.

Later, he and Jesse made lunch in the kitchen. Well, Luke made lunch, while Jesse leaned against the counter and watched.

"Luke, trust me. You don't want me to cook."

"Hey, I'm no Julia Child. I'm making sandwiches."

"Who?"

Luke stopped chopping a tomato and fixed Jesse with a glare. "Okay, I am not *that* much older than you!"

"I know. I'm kidding." Jesse giggled. "She's the bitchy one who just went to jail, right?"

"That's Martha Stewart and you know it."

Jesse's innocent expression slipped away and he laughed again. "Okay, okay." He reached over and grabbed a piece of cheese before Luke could stop him.

"Hey, watch your hands, or you might lose a finger." Luke playfully brandished the knife.

"I'd prefer it if you spanked me."

Luke's throat was suddenly dry, and he looked at Jesse with hooded eyes. "Would you now?"

"Um, I mean," Jesse stammered, his eyes wide. "I was just kidding."

Luke set the knife down, and in an instant had Jesse pinned against the counter. "Well, it's not such a bad idea." He licked the side of Jesse's throat slowly.

"Uhhhh ..." Jesse started breathing heavily as Luke squeezed his ass. Then Luke pulled him away from the marble counter and smacked his ass, making Jesse yelp. He stared at Luke for a second before bursting out laughing. Luke joined in and they were soon giggling helplessly between kisses.

When the doorbell rang, Jesse quickly extricated himself from Luke's arms. Luke kissed him again quickly before heading to the front door, opening it to find his mother. "Mom! Fancy seeing you here."

Stephanie smiled. "I was just in the neighborhood and...Luke, don't look at me like that, I *was* in the neighborhood. Susan Deravish is living over on Woodlawn Street now."

"Sure, sure, whatever you say, Mom." Luke kissed her cheek, smiling. He took a breath and said, "There's someone you should meet. Someone I want you to meet."

She smiled again. "That would be lovely."

Luke led her into the kitchen, where Jesse was making a mess of the cucumber. He shrugged. "I told you I can't cook."

"That's chopping, not cooking," Luke noted. "Jesse, this is my mother."

"Hello. I've heard a lot about you." She approached him with her hand out.

Jesse shook it, "I've heard a lot about you, too, Mrs. Rossovich."

"Oh, please, call me Stephanie."

"Okay. Stephanie." Jesse flushed and ran his fingers through his hair.

Luke had to take a deep breath himself and remember that everything was fine, that his mother wouldn't be judging them. It was surreal to be standing in his kitchen with his mother and his lover. He never thought the day would come. "Mom, can you stay for lunch?"

"Oh, no, I was just passing by. I don't want to intrude."

Rolling his eyes, Luke asked, "Since when?"

They all laughed, and Luke went back to making sandwiches before Stephanie shooed him away and finished them herself.

"YOUR MOM IS really cool." Jesse's head was on Luke's chest as they lounged on the couch later that night watching TV.

"Yeah, I guess she is."

"Do you think she likes me?"

"Yes."

Jesse raised his head. "How can you be so sure?"

"Because she told me when I walked her to her car."

"Really? What did she say?"

"That you seemed like a very nice young man."

"That's all?"

"And that you had a nice ass."

Jesse smacked Luke's stomach. "She did not!"

"Oh, wait, maybe that was Aaron." Luke tried not to laugh but failed.

"Very funny." Jesse settled down again, his hair tickling Luke's chin. "Did he really say that? About my ass?"

"Aren't we the little egotist?"

"Well, I did score the hottest guy on the ATP tour." Jesse grinned. "Well, *one* of the hottest."

"Oh, that's it." Luke rolled Jesse off the couch onto the carpeted floor, following close behind. He pressed his body down on top of Jesse's and pinned his arms. "*One* of the hottest? The Association of Tennis Professionals has no hotter player. Who the hell's hotter than I am? And if you say Koehler, you're history."

Jesse couldn't seem to keep a straight face. "Okay, I won't say Koehler. But Grankvist is pretty smokin'. Not to mention Scattergood."

"Scattergood? That Aussie himbo can't string together two sentences."

"I'm not interested in his vocabulary, Luke." Jesse waggled his eyebrows.

Luke shut him up with a kiss, and it didn't take long before they were pulling at their clothes, reaching for bare skin. Luke licked his way down Jesse's body, stopping to suck his nipples until Jesse moaned and bucked his hips up.

As he bypassed Jesse's cock and moved down his legs, Jesse groaned in frustration. "Luke, come on."

"Oh, I'm sorry. Did you want something?" Luke looked up from where his head rested on Jesse's inner thigh.

"You know what I want."

"Say it."

Jesse's fingers twisted in Luke's hair. "I want you to suck me." He licked his lips, adding, "And I want to suck you, too."

A shot of adrenaline went right to Luke's dick and he swiped his tongue up towards Jesse's cock. Shimmying around on the carpet until they were in the right position, he took Jesse into his mouth. Jesse started licking too, his tongue sliding up and down the ridge of Luke's shaft.

Soon they were both licking and sucking with abandon, and Luke was overwhelmed with sensations—the taste of Jesse in his mouth and the incredible feeling of Jesse swallowing him deeper and deeper, quickly getting the hang of it. Luke cradled Jesse's balls in his hand, massaging them lightly. He felt rather than heard Jesse's gasp of pleasure and before long, Jesse was shooting into his mouth.

Luke swallowed and when Jesse mimicked him, rolling Luke's balls in his hand, he went over the edge. They both caught their breath and eventually, Jesse shifted around until they were facing each other again. They kissed lazily, tongues tangy and salty.

"You still think I'm not the hottest guy on the tour?"

Jesse pondered it. "Hmm. Well, you might have some competition from me."

"Yeah, I just might," Luke agreed, pulling Jesse into his arms once more.

The next morning, Luke decided to go down early and cook up some breakfast. Jesse was fast asleep when he crept out of bed, and Luke didn't want to wake him. He hummed under his breath while he fried up some eggs and bacon. To hell with the diet for one day.

Back upstairs, Luke nudged open the bedroom door with his shoulder, a tray laden with food in his hands. He stopped dead in his tracks when he saw that Jesse was awake. Not only awake, but looking through the contents of the bottom drawer of Luke's bedside table.

Luke's throat went dry. He kept all the important things in there—things from before. Pictures, notes, mementos. All the memories of Nik that he could hold on to.

He must have made a sound, because Jesse suddenly looked up and dropped the photos he was holding as if they were on fire.

"Luke!" He scrambled up. "I wasn't...I was just ..."

"Looking through my things?" Luke's jaw clenched. He had no right.

Jesse's face flamed a bright red. "Yeah. Sorry."

Luke put the tray down on the bed. "Find anything interesting?"

"I'm sorry, I was looking for...well, I just shouldn't have been looking. It was wrong."

"What were you looking for?" Luke crossed his arms over his chest.

If possible, Jesse went even redder and mumbled something under his breath.

"What?"

"I said I was looking for toys." His eyes were downcast.

"Toys?" Luke asked, confused.

"You know," Jesse sighed, exasperated, "for sex."

Luke couldn't help but laugh. "You were looking for sex toys?"

"Yeah, I'm a huge pervert, okay?" Jesse looked anywhere but at Luke.

"Yeah, it's more than okay." Luke sighed, the anger drained away.

"But I found all these pictures." Jesse picked one up, and finally looked at Luke with uncertainty. "He was your coach. Nikolai Urmanov, right?"

Luke nodded. "Yeah."

"I remember when he died. It was awful."

Luke swallowed hard. It was surreal to talk to Jesse about it. "A drunk driver plowed into him head on. They said he died instantly." He felt the familiar prick of tears and his voice wavered. "He went out to pick up some groceries and just never came back. He was just…gone. No warning, no chance to say goodbye."

Jesse was silent for a few moments as he looked at the picture in his hand. "He was your boyfriend, wasn't he?"

Luke blew out a deep breath. "Yes."

"For how long?"

"Seven years. Not long after he started coaching me."

"I had no idea. Well, obviously. Wow, you guys sure hid it well. I never suspected a thing, even when I was having whack-off fantasies of you every night." Jesse stopped suddenly. "God, I'm sorry. I'm rambling." He quietly added, "You must have loved him a lot."

"Yeah. I did."

"And you've…you've just been alone since it happened?"

"I've picked up a guy at a bar here and there. But it was just sex. No sleeping over, no kissing, no…emotions." Luke's stomach fluttered and he cleared his throat. He couldn't seem to stop himself from talking.

"So that's why you freaked out that day at your house when I kissed you."

"Yeah."

"And then after what happened in the parking lot?"

"I meant what I said; it wasn't you. It was me."

Jesse carefully laid the picture down on the bed with the others and walked to Luke. "I'm sorry I snooped around. I don't want you to think that you can't trust me."

"It's okay." Luke waved his hand. "I know you didn't mean any harm. It's good…good that you know the truth. I should have told you before."

Jesse inched closer and slipped his arms around Luke's waist. "Yeah, you probably should have. But it's okay. I understand. I can't imagine how hard it must be."

"Yeah, it's not easy sometimes." Luke couldn't think of anything else to say, but he didn't have to. Jesse just hugged him tightly, pressing tender kisses to his shoulder. Luke hugged him back, feeling like some more weight had lifted from his shoulders.

They eventually sat down on the bed and Luke looked at the congealed bacon and eggs dispiritedly. "Breakfast in bed isn't looking so hot anymore."

Jesse bit his lip. "Shit, I'm sorry. You made me breakfast and everything."

"Well, I guess you'll just have to be punished," Luke arched his eyebrow. "Maybe we'll go toy shopping later."

Jesse giggled, kissing him soundly. Soon they stretched out on the bed, all thoughts of breakfast forgotten.

THE SKIES OVER Miami were heavy with rain, and all the players picked up the pace of the game, trying to finish it while they still could. Jesse and Luke were losing to a couple of guys from Sweden, and since he was into the semis in singles, Luke really didn't mind. Not that he'd admit that to Jesse. Jesse had lost in the first round to one of the top seeds.

"Fifteen-thirty," the umpire called out. If Jesse wasn't careful, his serve was going to be broken. He tossed the ball up and spun it over the net; one of their opponents put it away with a backhand that went just out of Luke's reach.

"Fifteen-forty."

Luke heard Jesse swear under his breath, which was rare for him. Usually no matter how badly things went, he kept his composure. Not that cursing was losing it—Luke swore at himself, his opponents, and the ump on a regular basis. He just tried to keep it inside his head. It worked sometimes.

Jesse double faulted on the next point and the game went to

their opponents. It didn't take long for the Swedes to finish them off, and as they packed up their stuff, the rain started to fall in big, fat drops. Luke began moving faster, cramming his things into his bag. But Jesse seemed to be in no rush and folded his towel carefully.

"Come on!" Luke called out over the sound of the rain that was fast becoming thunderous.

"Go on, I'll see you inside," Jesse said with a wave of his arm. The grounds crew was darting around them, covering up the court.

A crack of lightning brightened the sky and a huge clap of thunder followed moments later. "Jesse, come on!" Luke pulled his arm, urging him forwards.

Jesse yanked his arm away. "I'm fine, it's just a little rain."

"What's wrong?"

"We just lost, in case you haven't noticed!" Jesse angrily wiped rain from his face.

"So what?"

"Yeah, easy for you to say."

"What?" There was another strike of lightning. "This is ridiculous. Let's get inside."

"I said, go!"

"What is your problem?"

"My problem is that I lost in straight fucking sets in singles, and I just lost again." He threw his racquet into his bag. "It's frustrating, okay? You wouldn't understand."

"And why the hell not? You think I've never lost a match before?"

"Yeah, but you've won four Slams, Luke. I'm never going to get there if I keep playing like this." Thunder sounded ominously and the rain intensified.

"You'll get there. You will. But right now, let's get the hell inside before this thunderstorm turns into a hurricane."

"Fine." Jesse snatched up his bag, and they both hurried inside. Due to the rain, the locker room was crowded and they couldn't talk privately. They tried not to be seen too much together in public, afraid that their closeness would soon become apparent. On the court they made an effort to only slap hands on big points. Couples often unconsciously gave themselves away when the normal barriers of personal space were eroded by intimacy.

The last thing Luke needed was someone figuring out their secret.

Jesse seemed to take a long time changing out of his wet clothing, and Luke tapped his foot with impatience. When Jesse was ready, they walked quietly through the building towards the cars, with drivers ready to take them to the destination of their choice. The tournament provided courtesy transportation to and from the matches for the players, but Luke almost wished they didn't. He wanted to comfort Jesse, but he couldn't do that if they left in separate cars.

"I think I'm just going to go back to my room for a while," Jesse said.

"So now you're mad at me?"

"No, I'm mad at myself. I'm sorry I took it out on you."

"It's okay, I understand."

A tournament worker saw them coming and she approached them in the lobby with a professional smile. "I'll call for two cars right away, but I'm afraid it may take a few minutes due to the weather."

"That's okay; we're staying at the same hotel. We can share a car," Luke replied. It wasn't much, but at least they could ride back to the hotel together.

"Are you sure you don't mind?"

He smiled and said, "Of course not," while Jesse nodded absently. The woman scurried off to make the call.

Jesse headed outside, stopping under the large awning outside the door. Luke joined him and they watched the rain in silence.

Finally Jesse said, "I just want to be alone for a few hours, okay?"

"Sure." Luke shrugged.

"It's not you."

Luke barked out a laugh. "That sounds familiar."

"Yeah, well, I mean it. I just need to be depressed for a while."

"Jesse, come on."

"Please, just let me be. I'm frustrated with myself. And I don't want to take it out on you."

Luke nodded as a car pulled up. They slid into the roomy back seat after stowing their tennis bags in the trunk. The driver headed for their hotel, windshield wipers beating furiously against the rain. Luke was relieved when the man flipped on a radio station, cutting the thick silence. Tinny bubble-gum pop came out of the speakers, a young girl singing about how love had done her wrong.

Luke made sure that the driver was focused on the road—which he was, due to the torrential rain—and inched his hand across the leather seat under the cover of the Top Spin jacket he had tossed down. Jesse's fingers were cold and Luke squeezed, his palm warm on the back of Jesse's hand.

A sigh escaped Jesse's lips and he turned his hand over, threading their fingers together. They didn't look at each other, but held on tightly as they moved over the rain-soaked streets.

CHAPTER TEN

"**U**GH. I'M GOING to be doing laundry all night." Jesse peeled his red-stained shirt over his head. The clay courts were murder on crisp tennis whites and one tumble onto the court lunging after a ball had covered Jesse's clothes in the thick red dust.

"No, the hotel staff will be doing laundry all night. That's what they get paid for." Luke lounged on Jesse's bed, flipping through a magazine.

"You may be able to afford to have everything done for you, but some of us aren't superstars, you know."

Luke frowned up at Jesse. "Are you having trouble with money?"

"No, it's fine, don't worry." Jesse finished stripping and went into the bathroom, turning on the shower.

Tossing the magazine aside, Luke followed. He leaned against the counter and watched Jesse through the sliding glass shower doors. "Look, the only reason we're getting two rooms is for appearances, so why don't I just pay for both of them. We stay together anyway."

"Forget it; I should never have said anything."

"Well, I don't want to forget it."

Jesse groaned and stuck his head out of the shower, sliding one of the doors open. "Luke, seriously. It's fine. I have the money. It's just sometimes you act like everyone has multimillion-dollar endorsements."

Luke felt a flush of shame and thought of Mike, slugging away trying to make enough money to pay off the mortgage on his house. "Yeah, you're right. Sorry."

"It's okay. I'm just being bitchy because I lost in the second goddamned round." Jesse shifted back under the water, closing his eyes.

"You and me, both. Christ, I hate clay." The Rome Open was a big stop on the tour and good practice for the French. Not that Luke expected it to really make a difference. The clay slowed down his bullet of a serve, his big weapon. A teenager from Argentina who would probably go on to win, knowing Luke's luck, had beaten him. Jesse had fallen to a Russian journeyman who had barely eked out a victory. Jesse's chances were better than Luke's in Paris, his game more suited to the clay.

"So now we've got almost a week to kill until Hamburg," Jesse said. "Jeff wants me to pack up and be ready to leave in the morning for Germany since we're not bothering with doubles on clay. Practice, practice, practice. Sucks, because I've never had the chance to just hang out in Italy. All I ever get to see are airports, hotels, and tennis courts."

Luke opened up a towel and rubbed Jesse down when he emerged from the shower, making Jesse purr like a cat. Luke smiled and kissed his forehead. "Tell Jeff you need a couple of days."

"To do what?" Jesse grinned.

Luke shrugged and tried to keep the smile from his mouth. "Nothing special."

THE LIGHTS OF Venice shone across the Grand Canal and the

gondolier pointed out various sights as they sailed along. Dinner had been spectacular, and the pasta was sitting comfortably in Luke's stomach, the wine singing in his veins.

A four-hour train ride and they were a world away from the tour and all the stresses that came along with it. Luke was fairly certain the gondolier hadn't recognized him, so he looped his arm over Jesse's shoulders.

"This is, like, so much better than practicing." Jesse snuggled close.

"I'm not sure Jeff would agree."

"Well, what he doesn't know won't hurt him. It's not my fault I came down with food poisoning and missed my flight to Hamburg. And that I'll have to be in bed for the next two days."

"Mmm. These things happen." Luke's lips found Jesse's neck.

They sailed along in contented silence until the Rialto Bridge came into view. "Wow. Luke, it's amazing."

Whistling softly, Luke agreed. "Let's get out and walk across it." He'd never been to Venice before either and wanted to take in as much as he could. He paid the gondolier and they strolled along the canal, looking in the windows of shops selling blown Murano glass and other specialties of the region.

They ventured into one store and tried on Venetian masks, brightly colored in hand-painted detail.

"Let's buy them," Jesse said.

"What are we going to do with carnival masks?"

Jesse plucked Luke's from his hand and took it to the clerk along with his own. "Wear them?"

Luke's eyebrow shot up. "Hmm, that could be fun," he murmured.

Jesse grinned over his shoulder and indicated to the clerk that they didn't need wrapping. "We're wearing them now." He collected his change and thanked the man in Italian.

Outside the store, Jesse reached behind Luke's head and attached his mask. "Jesse, aren't we going to look a little...out of place wearing masks?"

Jesse fastened his own and wound his arms around Luke's waist. "The locals will just think we're annoying American tourists. Annoying American tourists they can't recognize." He pressed their lips together and Luke saw the wisdom of his idea.

Holding hands, they walked to the Rialto Bridge. A few people looked askance at them, but most just went on their way. The bridge was made of steps that rose above the canal to a peak in the middle and then back down the other side. At the top, they looked out over the water, arms around each other. The night air was cool and crisp, and Luke felt utterly content.

"Don't you wish it could always be like this?" Jesse asked.

"Well, we could always relocate to Venice to train."

"You know what I mean."

Luke glanced over, Jesse's serious eyes peering back from beneath his mask. "I'm not sure I do."

Jesse leaned in close and kissed him softly. "Like *this*. Out with you in public. Holding hands, being us."

"Yeah, well, in a perfect world, it would be nice."

"Sometimes I think maybe it's us who make such a big deal out of it. Maybe people wouldn't care as much as we think."

Luke snorted. "You're kidding, right? Jesse, if you think I'd have the endorsements I do if the world knew I was queer, you're out of your mind. Arnie Lachance wouldn't be my agent and I wouldn't have ever had my face on a cereal box."

"But you're an amazing player. If you win Slams, it's not like anyone can take that away from you."

Luke snorted. "Yeah, but they can make my life hell. Yours too. Think it would be fun in the locker room if the guys on tour knew the truth? Those macho assholes wouldn't let us off easy."

"Not everyone's like that, Luke."

"God, sometimes you really are young."

Jesse pulled away and stared at Luke. "Fuck you." He turned on his heel and walked back down the bridge, taking the stairs quickly.

Luke cursed under his breath and followed, tearing the mask off his face. He caught up to Jesse on a small street and pulled him into an alleyway. Jesse's mask was gone, too, and his eyes blazed.

"Careful, Luke. Someone might see us together and figure out the horrible truth."

"Damn it, would you stop? You know I'm right. We have to keep this a secret for the sake of our careers. Don't you think I wish things were different?"

"Things *can* be different. It would be hard, but it's not impossible."

"Jesse …" Luke took him by the shoulders gently, rubbed his hand up the back of his neck. "We'd be living under a microscope. We'd barely be able to concentrate on the game, let alone each other. I really do wish things were different. That I could shout it from the rooftops how wonderful you are. But I can't."

Jesse relaxed in his arms finally and leaned his forehead against Luke's. "You're right. I know that." He kissed him softly and smiled. "So, you think I'm wonderful, huh?"

"Yeah, I might," Luke chuckled. "But your ego's getting a bit big these days."

"Almost as big as yours."

They laughed and kissed and soon Luke had Jesse pressed up against the wall in the narrow alleyway. He sank to his knees and undid Jesse's jeans, taking his hardening cock into his mouth. Jesse moaned and his fingers ran through Luke's hair, holding his head lightly as Luke started moving up and down.

He sucked Jesse deep into his throat, humming softly at the same time. Jesse gasped and tightened his fingers in Luke's hair. By the time Jesse came, Luke was sure he'd lost quite a few hairs and his knees creaked when he lifted himself from the stone road.

However, he couldn't stop smiling as he kissed Jesse and they refastened their masks. With another kiss, they headed off to Piazza San Marco, hand in hand.

HOURS LATER, LUKE woke in the wee hours of the night. He rubbed his face blearily, not sure what had disturbed his slumber. He reached out for Jesse, but the bed was cold. Suddenly he was wide awake as he heard a low groan coming from the bathroom.

"Jess?" Luke padded over to the bathroom door and knocked softly.

"I'm fine, go back to sleep," Jesse croaked.

He didn't sound fine, and Luke opened the door, blinking into the harsh light. Curled on the bathroom floor in his track pants, Jesse was pale and shivering. "Jesus! What happened? What's wrong?" He knelt down, his palm moving to Jesse's forehead. "You're burning up."

"This is what I get for lying about having food poisoning," Jesse groaned. "Karma in action. It's a good thing I'm a quiet puker. Or maybe you're just a heavy sleeper."

"You're babbling." Luke put his arm under Jesse's shoulders and hauled him into a sitting position. He reached up to the sink and filled a glass with water, keeping one hand on Jesse's shoulder so he didn't slide back down to the floor again. "Drink this."

Jesse coughed and moaned but managed to keep some of the water down. But not for long. "Oh, god," he muttered as he turned to the toilet. He heaved repeatedly as Luke rubbed his back. When he was finished, he collapsed and laid his head in Luke's lap.

"Maybe I should call the hotel doctor." Luke stroked Jesse's hair gently.

"No, I'll be fine. Just a stomach bug or something." His eyes fluttered closed.

He was weak and small in Luke's arms and Luke's heart beat double time in his chest. "I don't want to take the chance; this could be serious."

A faint smile tugged at Jesse's lips, but his eyes remained closed. "You're worried about me."

"Of course I am!" Christ, Jesse looked like death warmed over. Maybe it was more than just a bug. Luke's mind whirled with the possibilities.

"It's just...nice." Jesse snuggled closer and pressed his lips to Luke's stomach. "Stop worrying, I'll be fine."

"Well, you're not sleeping in the bathroom." Luke scooped him up into his arms and took him back into the bedroom, lowering him to the mattress. Then he took the trashcan from the desk and brought it over to Jesse's side of the bed. "If you need to be sick again you don't have to get up."

"Mm-hmm." Jesse drifted back into an uneasy sleep.

When sunrise filled the room with a warm glow, Luke was still awake, Jesse's fevered skin flush against his chest.

"WOULD YOU STOP fussing?" Jesse batted Luke's hand away from his forehead.

"I am not *fussing*. I just want to make sure your temperature's staying down."

The cab driver kept his eyes on the road towards the airport. He seemed more interested in the pop song he was singing along to, rather than Jesse and Luke. The traffic was moving quickly— so quickly that Luke wondered if they'd extended Germany's Autobahns to Italy as well.

"I just slept for, like, sixteen hours or something. At least I'll be well rested for practice later."

"You're going to practice today?"

"Jeff said the court is booked if I'm feeling up to it."

"Just remember you've got a layover in Rome before you make it to Germany." Since Jesse was never supposed to be in Venice, he couldn't very well arrive on a flight from the city.

"I feel better. I haven't puked since yesterday and I'm not seeing spots. So don't worry, okay?"

"When were you seeing spots?"

Jesse rolled his eyes and smiled. "I wasn't, it's just…a figure of speech, or something."

"No, it's not."

"Yes, it is."

"Since when? Since when is 'seeing spots' a figure of speech?"

Laughing, Jesse shrugged. "I don't know, I didn't get a memo or anything."

"No? No memo?" Luke reached over and tickled Jesse's ribs.

"Hey!"

They tussled briefly, Jesse giggling as he tried to squirm away. Luke was about to go in for a second attack when he glanced at the rearview, meeting the driver's eyes. The laughter died in his throat and his hands fell into his lap. Jesse looked at him quizzically, just for a second. Then he cleared his throat and shifted away, his gaze turning out the window.

As they neared the airport, the driver turned down the radio and asked them again which airline. When they pulled into the terminal, he asked them if they'd miss Italy. Luke could feel Jesse's eyes on him as he said that yes, he would miss Italy very much.

STEVE ANDERSON TOOK a swig of water and rolled up his shirtsleeves. "Can we get a fan or something in here? It's hotter than hell."

His producer told him they were working on fixing the A/C, and Steve continued grumbling. Then the players were back on court from the changeover and he was back on the air.

"The players are evenly matched at one set apiece," Steve said. "Although they're not so evenly matched when you look at their records on clay. This surface just hasn't been kind to Rossovich over the years. He's a great champion, but I think the one year he made the semis here at Roland Garros might be the farthest he's going to go."

His partner in the booth agreed, rattling off some statistics for both players. However, they were broadcasting on an American network, and the public wanted to at least hold out some hope that their favorite players could pull the upset. Therefore, Steve added, "But Luke did get to the quarters last week in Hamburg, so there's hope yet. Maybe he can take this third set and pull ahead of Marcel Lopez."

Steve and his partner looked at each other and rolled their eyes. They'd be surprised if Luke Rossovich ever won another Slam in the twilight of his career, let alone the French Open.

CLOUDS CREPT ACROSS the Paris sky, threatening rain. Luke wiped his brow with the sleeve of his T-shirt and bounced the ball twice before going into his service motion. It had rained the day before, making the clay court even slower, and Luke's usually killer serves were turning into easy returns for his opponent.

Lopez blasted a backhand over the net and Luke ran for it, smacking a forehand return back. Luke had taken the first set, but Lopez had drubbed him in the second, winning it 6-2. They rallied back and forth, Luke finally winning on a forehand reach that had him sliding onto the clay court on his ass. He stood up and brushed himself off as the crowd applauded.

He was popular no matter where he went in the world, and shouts of "Allez, Luke!" could be heard throughout the stadium. It was the round of sixteen, meaning that sixteen players were left in the draw. Luke had been seeded seventh in the tournament due to his world ranking, but at Roland Garros, that didn't mean much. He'd been in the top ten in the world for the past nine years, but on clay, there were dozens of men who could beat him.

He lunged for a passing shot and missed. Lopez pumped his fist, a break of serve within his grasp. Luke wiped his brow again and huffed out a breath before bouncing the ball. He threw it up into the air and hoped for the best.

Later as he unwound under a hot shower, Luke replayed the match in his head. The unforced errors, the double faults, the missed opportunities. Intellectually he knew he probably just wasn't destined to win the French. Still it stuck in his craw that he failed, year after year.

Jesse was on court and Luke headed over after his shower to see how it was going. He was surprised to see that Jesse had taken the first set handily. He was playing damn well, and pride surged through Luke. Jesse had spent a lot of time training with Jeff and it was paying off.

Luke scanned the stands for the coach, finally spying his balding head halfway down the bleachers. Jesse was playing on one of the smaller courts, neither he nor his opponent big enough names to rate the big show courts. Luke made his way down to Jeff.

"Hey," he said, taking the empty seat beside him. The stands were barely half full, and the closest spectators were a few rows down.

Jeff smiled, but Luke noticed a tightness there. "Hey, Luke."

"He's playing damn well today."

"Sure is."

"Guess all those long days of practice in Hamburg paid off."

Jeff shrugged. "Yep, I guess so. Either that or it was the vacation you boys took to Venice. It was Venice, right?"

"Look, he needed a break. So he wasn't really sick. It all turned out okay." Luke's heart hammered in his chest and he forced a smile. "I guess Jesse's not too good at keeping a secret."

"Oh, he is. But it's pretty hard to pull the wool over my eyes." Jeff looked at him for a long moment, then peered back out at the court. "Venice is nice this time of year."

"Yeah, May's a good time to go," Luke agreed awkwardly. His face felt hot, and he shifted in his seat.

"Romantic city."

The coil of dread in Luke's stomach grew large. "I guess."

Jeff's gaze stayed on Jesse on the court, chasing down returns. "Do you love him?"

"What?" Luke croaked out.

"Because he loves you. He's a good kid, and I don't want you fucking with his head. If this is just about getting your rocks off, you'd better tell him that."

"Look, Jeff, I'm not sure where you got the idea that there was something—"

"Spare me. There's something going on—you know it, I know it, and if you're not damn careful, the whole world will know it. Think about his career. Yours is almost over, and you've had your fair share of glory. You think he'll last on the tour with everyone knowing he's a fag?"

Anger flared and Luke gritted his teeth. "Don't call him that."

"That's a word he's going to hear a lot if this all comes out."

"Does he know? That you know?"

"No, and he needs to focus on his game right now. He doesn't need any more distractions. So I'm just going to keep on pretending that I'm oblivious." Jeff finally looked at him again. "Look, I've got no problem with it, okay? But other people will, and you two had better be careful."

"We will be. We are."

Nodding, Jeff said, "Keep it that way." Jesse broke the other player's serve and Jeff stood up and cheered, clapping loudly. Luke stayed in his seat, silent.

"OH, MY GOD, I can't believe it!" Jesse jumped onto the bed, bouncing for a moment before he settled down on the duvet, arms and legs outstretched. "I'm in the quarterfinals. The quarterfinals of a Grand Slam!"

Luke smiled and leaned back against the door of the hotel room. "You played great today."

"I know! I did, didn't I? This is like, oh, my god, so amazing."

"Yeah, it is."

Jesse's smile faltered. "I'm sorry you lost. I'm being really obnoxious, aren't I?"

"No, no. You should enjoy this. You deserve it." Luke smiled at him reassuringly. "You should celebrate."

"Yes, we should." Jesse fixed him with a seductive look. "So what are you doing all the way over there?" He raised his hand, beckoning to Luke.

"You shouldn't tire yourself out." Luke heard Jeff's warnings over and over again in his head like a tune he couldn't stop humming. Maybe some distance from Jesse was wise.

Jesse blinked at him in surprise. "You...you don't want to?"

"It's not that. I just want you to be at your best."

As he sat up, the smile faded from Jesse's face. "Why are you acting so weird?"

"I'm not," Luke scoffed.

"Yes, you are. You're all...uptight or something."

"It's just been a long day."

"It is...are you upset that you lost? And I didn't?"

Luke rolled his eyes and strolled over to the minibar, grabbing a beer. "*No.* I'm not jealous."

"Then what?"

"Nothing. It's nothing." Luke gulped down some beer and slammed down the bottle. "You're right—let's celebrate." In a few movements, he had Jesse pinned back against the bed, arms over his head.

They kissed and stripped quickly, moving together in a tangle of limbs, Luke thrusting inside Jesse as they both moaned in pleasure. They were careful about their secret, Luke told himself— he was just being paranoid because of Jeff. There was no reason to worry.

He lost himself in Jesse and hoped it was true.

CHAPTER ELEVEN

HEATHROW AIRPORT WAS a madhouse, as always. Luke and Jesse had caught different flights, Luke reminding him that they couldn't be seen together too much. The British media was famed for its salaciousness, and if they caught a whiff of scandal, they'd be all over Jesse and Luke.

As it was, Luke had flashbulbs going off in his face as he headed to his car, the driver leading him through the crowds. Fans shouted his name, and he gamely waved to them, smiling and playing his role.

Finally ensconced in the back of the luxury car, he relaxed, tipping his head back against the seat. Jesse had lost in the quarterfinals of the French, and now both of them were headed to London's Queen's Club for a tournament on grass that served as a tune-up for Wimbledon.

The car wound its way through the busy streets of London towards Luke's hotel. They'd be in London for three weeks, and normally Luke would have rented a townhouse in a quiet part of the city. It was nice to have some privacy and a sense of normalcy—by the time he returned to the States following Wimbledon, he would have been gone for two months.

However, with Jesse part of the picture, they needed to stay in the same hotel so if they were seen together, there was a logical explanation. He wished it could be different, but as Nik used to say, "If wishes were trees, we'd all be drinking vodka."

Luke smiled at the memory. Nik loved to mangle phrases to make his own sayings to go along with the Russian ones Luke didn't understand. He shut his eyes and remembered, the city slipping by unnoticed. He still felt a stab of guilt when he thought of Nik, but as time went on, it lessened.

Sometimes, Luke didn't know whether to be happy or sad about that.

The hotel was big and well appointed, home to many players during The Championships, the simple moniker the British used for Wimbledon, as if no other identifier was needed. Luke supposed it wasn't. For all the glory and prestige of the other Slams, it was Wimbledon that held the most magic, the most history.

As a three-time winner, Luke was huge with the fans and as he stepped from the car, more cameras flashed. He took a few minutes to sign autographs for the waiting crowd, who screamed and grinned and bounced up and down. Luke could never really understand why they were so excited to see him, but the attention flattered him. He was only human.

His room was large and plush, and he wasted no time in flopping down on the bed. His eyes drifted shut, the late afternoon sun warm on his face through the big window. The flight had been a short one, but there was something about travel that always made him drowsy.

He awoke some time later to a quiet knock at the door. He ignored it at first, slipping back easily into his dreams. But it sounded again, and with a groan, he heaved himself up. He opened the door to find Jesse, bouncing on his toes and looking up and down the hallway.

"It's about time." He pushed Luke back into the room and closed the door behind them. "Someone could have seen me, you know."

Luke stretched back out on the bed, covering his head with a pillow. "What time is it?"

"Time to order room service. I'm starving. You must be, too."

Yawning, Luke agreed, "Come to think of it, I am."

"You want the usual?" Jesse flipped through the menu, perched on the side of the bed.

"Sure. Wait, what's my usual?"

"Chicken breast, baked potato, whatever vegetables they have. They've got a rosemary chicken thing; it should fit the bill."

Jesse ordered their dinner while Luke ruminated on the fact that Jesse knew him well enough to order his dinner. A smile tugged at his lips.

"What?" Jesse looked down at him.

"Nothing, I was just thinking."

"Uh-oh, we all know how dangerous that can be."

"You little shit." Luke laughed, hauling him down across his body on the bed.

"I certainly am." Jesse kissed him.

"How long for the food?"

"Half an hour. Long enough?" He ground his hips down suggestively.

"Hmm. Maybe we should wait. I don't want to rush."

Jesse slid off him, curling up to his side. "No, we wouldn't want that."

"What time's your practice court booked for tomorrow?"

"Way too early. But you know Jeff." He deepened his voice, imitating him. "The early bird gets the worm."

"Hey, you got to the quarters in Paris; I guess you shouldn't knock it."

Jesse snorted. "Yeah, and then I lost 6-1, 6-0, 6-1. In, like, fifty minutes."

"Hey, at least you avoided the triple bagel, right?"

"Yeah, those two games I won are something to be proud of."

Luke rolled over, resting his head on his hand as he peered at Jesse. "You know how amazing it is to get to a quarterfinal of a Slam in your third year on tour? Some guys work for years and never get that far. You're having a great year, so don't knock it."

"Okay, I won't." Jesse sighed. "I know you're right. I guess I'm just impatient. You were only a bit older than me when you won Wimbledon the first time."

"Yeah, and I didn't go to college. I'd been slugging away on the tour as a pro since I was barely eighteen. It takes time, Jesse."

"Okay, okay. You're right."

"Now you're talking sense." Luke smiled.

They ate dinner in front of the TV and a British comedy that Jesse found particularly funny. On the other hand, maybe it was the bottle of wine they were quickly working their way through. Luke cleared their plates and deposited them in the hallway for the cleaning staff.

"God, I am so full," Jesse complained as he lay down on the bed. "And I think I'm a bit drunk."

Luke collapsed beside him. "Mm-hmm."

They watched TV in contented silence and dozed off. Luke awoke just after midnight and stumbled to the bathroom, flicking off the TV and the overhead light as he went. When he returned to the bedroom, Jesse was awake and by the window, looking out over the city.

"It's so big. Looks like it just goes on forever. But in a different way than LA. You know what I mean?"

Luke pressed up behind him at the window, wrapping his arms around his waist. "Yeah, I know what you mean." He dropped a kiss on the back of Jesse's neck.

After a few minutes, Jesse turned in his arms and pressed kisses along Luke's jaw, moving to his ear. Their hands started to roam as their bodies reawakened, and they moved back to the bed. When Jesse pulled Luke's shirt over his head, Luke winced a bit at the twinge in his shoulder.

Jesse stopped and sat back on his heels. "You okay?"

"My shoulder's just a bit off today. I think I strained it yester-day."

Jesse rubbed Luke's shoulder tentatively. "Man, you've got a lot of knots back there."

"Tell me about it."

"Lie down on your stomach."

Luke didn't argue, and helped kick his jeans and underwear off. "Have any massage oil?"

"No, but there should be some moisturizer in the bathroom."

Jesse returned and straddled Luke's hips in his underwear. "Aveda, huh? I didn't know guys used moisturizer."

"What kind of gay man are you?"

Jesse smacked Luke's ass. "The kind that's going to give you a massage, so shut it."

Jesse worked the moisturizer into Luke's sore muscles, and Luke purred in satisfaction. Jesse was good with his hands and as he moved down his body, Luke felt like his skin was glowing.

As his fingers splayed over Luke's ass, Jesse's lips were suddenly there, blowing a stream of air over Luke's hole.

"Fuck," Luke moaned, his dick already hard beneath him from the massage.

Jesse's tongue darted out and he licked up and down the crack of Luke's ass, flicking over his hole and finally probing inside. Luke could feel Jesse's breath hot against him and he pushed back against his tongue. "Yeah, just like that."

After another minute, Luke was rubbing his cock against the mattress, trying to create the necessary friction. He finally groaned and lifted his head up, turning to look over his shoulder. "Get the stuff from my bag." He rolled on his side to wait.

Jesse complied with a nod and shucked his briefs on his way back to the bed. He pressed the condom and lube into Luke's hand. "How do you want me?" he asked, teeth tugging on Luke's ear.

"Inside me."

Jesse's eyes widened in surprise. "Really?"

"Yes, really. I may be a top, but I still like having someone else drive the train once in a while." He kissed Jesse thoroughly, until they were both panting. "Now fuck me." He hadn't bottomed for anyone since Nik, but it felt right.

He rolled back over, grabbing a pillow and shoving it beneath his hips as he spread his legs. He heard the lube open, and then Jesse's finger was pushing inside him, opening him up. He added another finger and Luke moaned at the sensation.

There was a tear of foil, and then Jesse was on top of him, pressing himself hesitantly into Luke's hole. "You need to push harder," Luke told him.

"I don't want to hurt you."

Luke looked back over his shoulder and lifted his ass. "You won't. I promise."

Emboldened, Jesse pushed further inside him, and Luke felt that old familiar stretching, the pleasure and pain mixing together as one as Jesse moved further in. Finally, he was there, his hips against Luke's ass, breath coming in jagged inhalations.

"Oh my god," he whispered. "You feel so good." Kissing the back of Luke's neck, Jesse grasped his hand on the mattress. He took a few deep breaths and Luke knew he was trying to get back under control. When he did, he started thrusting in and out a bit, getting a feel for the motion.

Soon he had it down and he drove back and forth, hitting just the right place to make Luke want to scream with pleasure. There was nothing quite like getting fucked sometimes, and he rocked back against Jesse, meeting his thrusts. He lifted his hips, sliding his hand beneath his body to stroke his cock as Jesse started pumping faster, his moans getting louder.

Then Jesse was coming, his hand still clutching Luke's as his hips jerked and his body shook. Luke gave his dick one more hard tug before he came, his ass clenching and making Jesse grunt and spasm again before he collapsed onto Luke's back.

"Oh my god," Jesse rasped. "That was amazing." He kissed Luke's sore shoulder tenderly, his fingers smoothing over Luke's skin.

"Yeah, it was."

Jesse pulled out and Luke winced a bit. He'd have a few new sore muscles in the morning, but as Jesse curled up beside him, a huge smile on his face, Luke didn't give a damn.

JESSE RAISED HIS hand for a high-five and Luke slapped his palm accordingly. They were in the semifinals of the Queen's Club tournament and damned if they weren't giving the good old Stifflers a run for their money. Luke was sure he and Jesse wouldn't win, but at least they'd taken a set off the brothers.

He and Jesse fought hard, and the crowd grew as the match progressed. Doubles didn't always draw many fans, but word spread quickly at a tournament when there was a good match to watch.

The brothers did end up taking it in the third, 7-5. The two teams shook hands at the net before moving to their chairs to gather up their equipment.

"We came pretty close." Jesse zipped up his hoodie.

"Damn right. Maybe next time we'll beat the bastards."

"Hey, we heard that," Tom Stiffler called out good-naturedly from the other side of the umpire's chair.

"I know," Luke said. "You were supposed to."

"You Americans, always so cocky!"

"Whatever, mate, you Aussies are just as bad!" Jesse said,

laughing.

"Bloody oath we are! We're the best, after all." Tom's brother, Ian, grinned.

They all headed back to the clubhouse, going through the players' tunnel into the locker room. As they ambled along, Tom said, "Sorry to see you go out in the semis to Jennings, Luke."

"Yeah, me too," Luke replied.

"But you're looking good for Wimbledon, mate," Ian said. "I'd love to see you knock Koehler off his perch."

"Wouldn't we all," said Tom.

They all nodded their agreement. "You know, it's not that he wins so much, it's that he's such a prick about it," Jesse noted.

Ian replied, "Ain't that the truth. Hey, good on ya for getting to the quarters in Paris. You're having a good year, aren't you? Your ranking must be moving up."

"Yeah, I'm at seventy-nine this week."

They arrived at the locker room and started undressing for the shower. Luke kept his eyes averted, since it seemed just the sight of Jesse's tight little body could make him hard of late.

"I'm at two hundred and fifty in singles." Ian laughed. "So you're doing a hell of a lot better than me."

"Yeah, but I'm not a doubles specialist like you guys," Jesse said.

"True, true. And we are the best in the world. Have we mentioned that?" Tom grinned.

Luke put on a falsely interested voice. "Really? Oh, *do* tell us more."

They all laughed together, joking and taking a strip off each other as they headed to the showers. Despite the earlier loss to Jennings, Luke found himself feeling positive, and he looked forward to the fortnight to come.

THE MERCURIAL BRITISH weather played havoc on the first day of Wimbledon, causing repeated rain delays. Players hung out in the lounge, playing cards, watching TV, reading, and trying to figure out when the best time to eat was, hoping the skies wouldn't suddenly clear. There was nothing worse than being called back on court with a full stomach.

Luke put down his book and casually glanced across the lounge to where Jesse was playing poker with a few of the guys. He didn't seem to be winning, but he was smiling nonetheless. Luke found himself smiling, too.

"See something you like?"

Luke's head snapped around at the sound of the sneering German accent. Koehler. He lowered himself into the armchair next to Luke's with a feline grace that belied his size and strength.

Luke raised his eyebrow and nodded towards Rina Depp, the beautiful girlfriend of Jean-Paul Riel. Rina lingered by Riel's side, whispering something in his ear where they sat just off to the side of Jesse's card game. "Can't help myself. She's a stunner."

"Mmm. Yes, stunning." Koehler smiled, and Luke felt a shiver go up his spine. "Beautiful hair. Like the color of gold."

"You must need glasses, Stein, my old friend. Her hair's black."

Koehler smiled again, never taking his eyes from Luke's. "Ah, so it is."

Luke looked back down at his book, eyes moving over the words, but not concentrating. Koehler was making him nervous.

"Did you have a good time in Italy, Luke?"

Luke didn't look up. "Not really. I lost early."

"But you paid a visit to Venice afterwards, no?"

"Where did you hear that?" Luke's heart pounded, and he kept his eyes on his book.

"Oh, around. Wonderful city, isn't it?"

"Mmm."

Just then, an announcement crackled over the loudspeakers, telling them that the rain had stopped and the courts were being uncovered. Luke snapped his book shut. "It's been nice catching up with you, Stein." He hurried off as fast as he could without making it look like he was running away.

That night, he paced in his room, waiting for Jesse to arrive. Finally, there was a knock, and he ushered Jesse in.

"We've got a problem," Luke told him.

The smile evaporated from Jesse's face and his hands froze on Luke's hips. "What happened?"

"Koehler knows we went to Venice together."

"What? How?"

"I don't know. Did you tell anyone?" Luke resumed pacing.

"No! Of course not."

"Well, someone told him."

"Well, it wasn't me."

Luke's tone was sharp. "Then who was it?"

"Are you accusing me?" Jesse sputtered. "Why the hell would I tell that asshole?"

"No, I'm not accusing you." Luke sighed and his voice softened. "I know you wouldn't tell anyone. I'm sorry; I didn't mean to get angry with you."

"It's okay." Jesse wrapped his arms around Luke and kissed him. "We'll just have to be careful, right?"

"Right."

"And we already are. I'm sure he's just trying to psyche you out. He probably doesn't know anything, Luke."

"Maybe not." Luke leaned his cheek against Jesse's head and enjoyed the feel of him in his arms, his distinctive scent filling his senses.

"So let's not worry about Stein Koehler."

Jesse stirred against him and they kissed, slowly at first, tongues and hands exploring leisurely. They stretched out on the bed and peeled their clothing away and as Luke's mouth moved across Jesse's stomach, he marveled at how he couldn't get enough of him.

What he'd had with Nik had been wonderful, but he felt like what he felt for Jesse was getting stronger by the day, possessing him to a degree he'd never felt before. When they were apart, he missed him fiercely, and sometimes it scared him a little.

They rolled around on the bed, kissing deeply, bodies straining together. They both gasped for breath, Jesse on top of Luke, grinding his hips down. Luke groaned and decided it was time to get to it, or they'd be coming from humping each other alone.

He sat up and maneuvered Jesse onto his hands and knees, reaching for the lube and a condom. Jesse pushed back against his slick finger, spreading his legs further. He thought for a moment about what it would be like to just forget the condom and thrust into him, feel the burn of flesh on flesh. What it would be like to come inside him, feel himself spilling into Jesse's tight hole ...

"Christ," he muttered, taking a moment to catch his breath so he wouldn't come right there. Obviously condomless sex would be a decision they discussed together. One they had plenty of time for. Luke slipped the condom on and soon he was moving inside Jesse, hands tight on his slim hips.

"God, Luke," Jesse moaned.

"Is it how you used to imagine it would be?" Luke knew his ego didn't need any more boosts, but he couldn't resist asking.

"Better. So much better."

"You like my cock in your ass?"

"Yes, yes, god yes," Jesse murmured as they moved together, a steady rhythm punctuated by their gasps and moans.

A drop of sweat ran down Jesse's spine, and Luke bent to taste it, his tongue swiping upwards as he angled his hips to thrust deeper. "You're so tight," he grunted.

"Right there," Jesse gasped, and Luke started pistoning his

hips faster, hitting the same spot over and over again until Jesse was coming with Luke's name on his lips.

Luke came a moment later and waves of pleasure washed over him. Head thrown back, mouth hanging open, Luke rode the wave. When it subsided, he realized that he was clutching Jesse hard enough to leave bruises. He sat back on his heels and disposed of the condom quickly, returning to bed and covering Jesse's hips in slow, tender kisses.

"Mmm," Jesse murmured. He rolled over onto his back. His stomach was wet with splashes of his seed, and Luke licked him clean as Jesse caressed his hair. Luke shifted and spooned up behind, pulling Jesse close against his chest.

"It's all better than I ever imagined," Jesse whispered as they drifted off to sleep.

Luke agreed and squeezed him tightly. He wasn't sure when it had happened, but he never wanted to let go.

CHAPTER TWELVE

"DAMN," MIKE MADISON exclaimed as Luke's serve zoomed past him. "That rocket is on fire today."

Luke grinned. "Yeah, looking pretty good, huh?"

"You don't need me to tell you that. But I do anyway."

"That's what friends are for, Mike."

"You'd better appreciate it." Mike tossed a ball into play and they began rallying back and forth.

"I do, don't worry." Luke practiced his backhand, hitting the same shot repeatedly.

Their practice court was one of the small outside courts at the Wimbledon club. A sizable crowd gathered to watch since Luke was there. When he hit a particularly good shot, they applauded, and he waved his thanks.

"Let's take five," Mike suggested.

They met at their chairs and gulped some water. Luke took a bite of an energy bar.

"So you and McAllister seem to make a good team, huh?"

Luke nodded as he swallowed. "Yeah." He took another swig of water and added, "I guess."

"I've been playing doubles my whole career and I've never even been to a final. You guys are looking good."

"We've been lucky."

"Luck, schmuck," Mike scoffed. "He's having a good year.

You'd better watch out; he'll be winning Slams before long."

Luke smiled ruefully. "I'll be long retired. All those little aches and pains are getting bigger and bigger each year. I don't know how much longer I can keep it up. Or even if I want to."

"Yeah, I hear that. Shell and I were talking about me taking on a pro job at one of the clubs in LA. after this year. There are plenty of rich people to give lessons to. And I'll get to see her and the kids a lot more."

"Sounds like a plan."

"I guess." Mike sighed. "I don't know." He sighed again and waved his hand dismissively. "It's stupid, forget it."

"What?"

"I guess I just…all these years, I've been thinking that one day my shot will come. That everything will fall into place, the stars will align, and I'll win one of the big ones."

"It's not too late," Luke lied. Mike was a solid player, but he wasn't good enough. Never would be.

"Thanks for saying that, but you know it's never going to happen. I know it, Shell knows it, everyone in the world knows it. So why am I hanging on to this dream?"

"Because dreams are hard to give up. You can know something in your head, but your heart…it's a different story."

"Ain't that the truth?" Mike ran his hand through his hair and chuckled. "Well, I say we've had enough deep thoughts for the day, how about you?"

"Ready to get smoked again?" Luke grinned, trying to lighten the mood.

"As always." They laughed and played on.

AFTER PRACTICE AND a long shower, Luke headed back to the hotel. As the driver navigated the narrow streets, Luke tipped his head back against the seat and listened to the radio. The DJs talked about the latest gossip involving a British rock star and the hot new Russian girl on the tour. Tongues were always wagging at Wimbledon.

Back upstairs, Luke slipped the keycard to Jesse's room out of his pocket. Jesse had managed to lose the one he had for Luke's room, which Luke had teased him about earlier. He was learning that Jesse had a habit of misplacing things, and to his surprise, he found it rather endearing.

He closed the door quietly behind him and tiptoed towards Jesse, who was out on the balcony. Jesse turned around before Luke was even halfway there. "You're *so* not stealthy. You do know this, right?"

"Fine, fine," Luke said. "Ruin my fun."

Jesse threw his arms around him and they hugged for a moment before he propelled Luke backwards into the room. "The fun hasn't even started yet." He closed the drapes with a flourish, and then pushed Luke back onto the bed, straddling his hips.

"Hmm. And what did you have in mind?"

"I'm hungry," Jesse whispered, and as he slid to his knees and unbuttoned Luke's pants, Luke lay back and closed his eyes.

Life was good.

THE KNOCK ON the door was soft, yet urgent. Luke blinked blearily at the digital clock on the nightstand. It was barely past six in the morning and he grumbled under his breath as he stumbled to the door.

Jesse rushed past him, a bundle of nervous energy. "Close the door!" he hissed.

Luke complied, wiping the sleep from his eyes. "What's wrong? It's six o'clock in the morning."

Jesse paced back and forth, a newspaper clutched in his hands. "Jeff woke me up ten minutes ago. He showed me this." Jesse held out the paper.

The bottom of Luke's stomach fell away and he wavered on his feet as he read the headline. *GAY SHOCKER!* A grainy picture of Luke and Jesse in each other's arms dominated the rest of the page. "Jesus," Luke muttered.

"I don't know how they got that picture; they must have been watching us."

Luke peered closely at the photo. "We're on the balcony of your room. Christ, I knew we should have kept the curtains shut. Why did you have to go out there anyway?"

"Well, excuse me for getting a breath of air. You didn't have to follow me."

Luke's head spun, and he quickly went to his window and drew the curtains the rest of the way, shrouding them in darkness. "Fuck!" Anger raged through him and he tossed a vase at the wall, shattering it.

How could he have been so stupid? How?

"Luke, calm down. Maybe it's not so bad."

"Not so bad! Are you serious?" Luke flipped on the overhead light so he could see where he was pacing.

"Well, we're not kissing in the picture. We're hugging. It's not like friends don't do that."

"Guys don't hang out together and hug," Luke spat, picking up the paper once more. He skimmed the article, which claimed that he and Jesse had been carrying on a secret affair for months. Which was true, of course. It also called into question Luke's relationship with Nikolai, causing Luke to scrunch up the paper and whip it across the room.

All these years he'd been so careful, and it was all falling apart in a heartbeat. One moment of carelessness, and it was over.

"Jeff said he already knew. He was pretty cool about it, you know. Maybe it won't be as bad—"

"Yes, it will, Jesse. God, don't be so naïve."

Jesse didn't respond, just sat down on the bed, hands twisting in his lap. Luke continued pacing around the room like a caged animal, desperately trying to think of a solution, a way out. But there was nothing.

After a while, Luke turned on the TV with a sense of dread. Sure enough, they were all over the early morning news, the one picture showing up on every network, making tongues wag. Soon the phone in Luke's room began ringing off the hook. He ignored it.

Finally Jesse said, "So are we just going to hide in here all day?"

"You know the second we open that door, there's going to be dozens of reporters in our face. You should have just called me. Why did you come to my room?" Luke snapped.

"Because I wanted to tell you in person. Because I wanted to see you. My mistake." His voice trembled.

Luke sighed. He was being a real bastard. "I'm sorry." He reached out for Jesse, pulled him into his arms. "I know it's not your fault. I'm just angry at everyone." He kissed his forehead.

"So what do we do now? What should I say to everyone?"

"Say it isn't true. Say we're friends, and you were upset about something."

Jesse raised his head from Luke's neck. "But what?"

"Losing your match."

"It's not like I haven't lost in the first round before. I was playing Riel; it would have been a miracle if I'd won."

"Well, losing still sucks. We'll just say that after getting to the quarters in Paris, you had high expectations, blah, blah, blah."

"I guess." Jesse shrugged. "But I'm not sure if anyone will buy it."

"They'll buy it if we sell it. Stick to the story and deny everything."

Jesse nodded, and then bolted to his feet. "Oh my god. My parents. They probably already know."

Checking the clock, Luke said, "They've probably just gone to bed. Hopefully no one will call them until it's morning in California. You can call them first."

"And tell them what?"

"That you were upset about the Riel match. That there's nothing going on. Stick to the story, Jesse."

"But...I don't want to lie to them."

"For now it's the only way. We have no idea how they'll react, what they might say to the media if they know the truth."

"I'm sure they wouldn't say anything I didn't want them to."

"These are our careers we're talking about. We can't take the chance. What if your father freaks out and disowns you?"

"I'm sure he would never ..." He trailed off, eyes wide. "You really think he would do that?"

"I don't know. That's the point." Luke stood and placed his hands on Jesse's shoulders. "We have to keep the story straight." He cracked a grim smile. "So to speak."

Jesse tried to smile back but failed. "Okay."

Luke leaned in and kissed him softly. He rested their foreheads together and Jesse's arms snaked around his waist. "It'll be okay," Luke whispered. "They can't prove anything."

A sharp knock at the door had them jumping apart skittishly. Luke quickly donned a shirt and pulled a pair of jeans on over his underwear as there was another knock.

"It's Jeff. Open the door."

Jesse did, closing the door quickly once Jeff was inside. Jeff looked back and forth between them before speaking. "I've got hotel security keeping everyone off the floor, except for hotel guests staying on this hallway. Hopefully this way, they won't see you coming out of the same room."

Luke nodded. "Thanks, Jeff."

"No problem. Now what have you decided to do?"

Luke filled him in, Jesse nodding in agreement every so often. Jeff listened quietly. Finally he said, "If that's the way you want to play it. But you know that you'll have to watch every step you make from here on out."

"It's the way it'll have to be for now," Luke agreed.

"No more doubles. It'll be too nerve-wracking for both of you to be together for long periods of time in public," Jeff said.

"But...we almost won last week. We're getting really good." It was the first thing Jesse had said since Jeff had arrived.

Luke shook his head. "There's no way we can play together now. It would be like playing in a fishbowl; the British press would have a field day."

"Kid, you'll have to pull out, claim an injury. It'll be better this way. We can head back home as early as tonight. We'll get a flight out ASAP." Jeff put his hand on Jesse's shoulder and squeezed. "Don't give them any more material to work with, and hopefully this'll all die down by the time the tournament is over."

Jesse looked between Luke and Jeff and finally acquiesced. "Okay, if that's what you guys think is best."

Luke said, "I'd better have a shower and get out to the practice courts."

Jesse frowned. "But won't there be reporters everywhere? How are you going to concentrate?"

He shrugged. "I'm going to have to tune it out. This tournament's far from over, and I'm not being chased away."

"Just I am, I guess."

"Jesse, it's not like that. It'll be better for you to be back home. You and Jeff can get some good training in. Here you'll just be—"

"In the way?" Jesse finished.

Jeff cleared his throat. "I'll be out in the hall. Come out when you're ready to go, kid."

Luke waited until the door had closed before approaching Jesse, cupping his face in his hands. "Jess, you know this isn't what I wanted. You know I'd rather have you here." He kissed him. "God, I hate the thought of not seeing you. I'm going to miss you." Luke knew it was the truth.

Jesse sighed and leaned against him. "I'm going to miss you, too. So much."

They kissed, tongues gliding together, lips soft. Luke wished there was more time, wanted to undress him and make love to him for hours. Maybe they could just stay in the room forever, the outside world forgotten.

A commotion in the hallway put an end to that notion. They broke apart and stood stock still as they heard security guards arguing with reporters, the voices starting to fade as they moved away down the hall.

"I guess I'd better get out of here."

"Yeah. We can't see each other before you go, it's just too risky. It'll have to wait until I'm back home." He kissed Jesse again. "Look at the bright side, I could flameout in the next round and be home before you know it."

Jesse smiled. "I'll hope for the best, then."

Their gaze met for a long moment, both reluctant to part. Luke thought about how strange it would be to be alone again, his bed empty, even if it was just temporary. How much he'd miss the taste of Jesse's mouth, the feel of his body, the sound of his laughter. "Fuck it," he growled as he pulled him close.

Their mouths met hungrily and they pulled at each other, desperate to get close one more time. They stumbled to the bed, Jesse quickly moving onto his hands and knees, pulling his pants and briefs down just enough as Luke yanked his own pants down and slid on a condom.

He pushed into Jesse with a grunt, his hand moving to Jesse's mouth to stifle his loud groan. Luke knew it was rough and that

Jesse would feel it later, but he didn't care. Jesse panted, his head tipped back, mouth open as Luke thrust into him. Luke's lips fastened on the side of Jesse's neck, marking the pale skin there.

"Oh, god," Jesse murmured. "Harder, Luke, harder."

He gripped one of Jesse's shoulders and pounded into him, his balls slapping against Jesse's ass. He knew he wouldn't last much longer, so he reached around and found Jesse's leaking cock, giving it a few hard strokes. He felt Jesse seize up, and warm come splashed his hand as Jesse gasped his name.

Luke felt the tingle spread through his body and let himself go, shooting long and hard, filling up the condom. They both collapsed onto the bed, breathing hard. Jesse turned his head, and they kissed gently. Luke breathed him in, fingers moving through his soft, blond hair.

There was a knock at the door. "We'd better get going," Jeff said.

"Be right there," Jesse called out.

They kissed once more and got up, straightening their clothes, cleaning up as best they could. At the door, Luke kissed him one last time. "Just remember, they can't prove anything."

Jesse nodded. He looked at Luke for a long moment and then said "See ya," his smile tremulous. He opened the door and was gone.

Luke stood alone for a long time until the phone began ringing again. He pulled the cord from the wall.

HOTEL SECURITY MET Luke at his door and escorted him down to the back entrance of the hotel. As he walked through the kitchen, Luke tried to ignore the eyes of the staff trained on him. He strode confidently, paying no mind to the whispers and odd giggle that reached his ears.

Flashbulbs exploded at he scooted into the car and reporters ran down the alley. Luke kept his head down and pretended they weren't there. The driver was impassive as they made their way towards Wimbledon and didn't listen to the radio or attempt to make small talk. Luke was grateful.

The British press always had a field day during Wimbledon, printing the most lurid tales they could muster, accompanied by whatever revealing pictures they could find. They appeared in an even greater frenzy than usual, and as Luke got out of the car, all he heard was a cacophony of sound.

He refused to run, and walked calmly inside the clubhouse, ignoring the questions screamed in his direction, the manic camera shutters. Once inside, it seemed eerily quiet. A staff member approached with a frozen smile on her face.

"Mr. Rossovich."

"The one and only."

"There's quite a commotion surrounding you today," she noted.

"You don't say."

Her smile didn't fade and her clipped, British accent was nothing but polite. "Not to worry, we'll ensure that your match isn't disrupted by all this nonsense."

"Thank you." Luke smiled and continued down the hall to the locker room before he paused and turned back to her. "Because it is, you know. Nonsense."

"Of course! Silly gossip, Mr. Rossovich. We don't pay it any mind."

"Glad to hear it." Luke turned the corner and headed into the locker room. He was meeting Mike for a practice session, unless Mike had other plans. Luke hadn't heard from him, so he assumed they were still on. As the door closed behind him, silence suddenly enveloped the room, chatter ceasing as all eyes turned.

Luke looked around at his colleagues. His friends. Some of

them looked away; others peered at him with open disgust. Luke dug down deep inside himself and smiled widely. "You shouldn't believe everything you read." He strolled casually to a locker and dropped his bag.

If he pretended nothing was wrong, maybe they'd buy it.

Then Mike was there, standing by his side. "Don't worry, Luke. We know those newspapers are out to lunch. They can do anything with that Photoshop these days." He clapped Luke on the back. "Ready for me to kick your ass?"

"Ready as always." Luke smiled, genuinely this time. The locker room came to life once more, everyone going back about their business. Luke could still feel hot stares on his back, but he ignored them once more.

The officials kept the press away from their practice court, so Mike and Luke were able to get in a good session. Luke waited for Mike to ask about Jesse, about what was really going on, but he didn't. They just practiced as usual, as though the media weren't splashing that picture of Jesse in Luke's arms all over the world.

When they took a break, Luke found he couldn't think of anything to say. He hated lying to Mike, especially since Mike had always been a loyal friend. Always. Luke cleared his throat. He had to say something. Yet no words would come.

Finally, Mike put him out of his misery. "So, about that picture. About what they're saying …"

"Yeah?" Luke held his breath.

Mike was quiet for a moment. "You'd tell me if it were true, right? We've been friends all these years; it's not like it would matter. You'd tell me if you were gay."

"Of course." Luke's throat felt like sandpaper and his stomach churned.

"Because it wouldn't be a big deal. To be honest…I used to wonder sometimes. About you and Nik."

"You did?" Luke couldn't keep the note of surprise from his

voice.

Mike shrugged. "There was just something about the way you two were together. Not all the time, just once in a while. But you were dating Alex, and I figured I was just imagining things."

Luke was pretty sure he was going to throw up. He took a deep breath. "You weren't imagining things."

Mike blinked in surprise. "Wait, are you saying...you are? You're really gay?"

Luke nodded jerkily. "I am."

"Wow." He shook his head. "I thought I was being crazy. So you and Nik ..."

"Yeah."

"Wow." Mike was repeating himself.

"It doesn't change anything, right?" Luke's heart pounded double time in his chest.

"No, of course not." Mike picked up his racquet and smiled quickly. Maybe too quickly. "Doesn't change anything. Come on, let's play."

He headed back to his side of the court, and they practiced for a bit longer. Luke mechanically returned shots and tried to pretend that everything was normal. After practice, Mike said he had some errands to do, and they didn't go for their customary snack. Luke told himself not to read too much into it, but it was difficult.

Back at the hotel, he battled the urge to call Jesse's room. He wasn't sure what time Jesse was leaving; for all he knew, Jeff and Jesse had gotten a flight quickly and were already gone.

After an hour, Luke popped two sleeping pills and welcomed oblivion.

CHAPTER THIRTEEN

I T WAS ANOTHER day before Luke could contemplate checking his messages. Most were from reporters he had no desire to speak to, but then he heard his mother's familiar voice.

"Luke, it's Mom. I heard the rumors on TV and I saw the picture on the Internet. I'm sorry, sweetheart. I hope you and Jesse are doing okay. I hear that you're denying everything but...I don't know, dear. Maybe it's time to be honest. It's up to you and Jesse, of course. Whatever you decide, you know I'll support you. Call me when you can. I love you."

With a beep, the message was over. Luke wanted to call her, but he didn't need to hear any advice on how he should be honest. Not after the looks he'd received in the locker room and everywhere else he went. There was no way anyone would accept him the way he was.

He'd call her soon. Just not right now.

After deleting a few more messages from reporters practically salivating at the thought of a comment from him, there was a message from Aaron.

"Hey, Luke. Obviously, I've heard the news. Hope you're doing okay, and call me anytime if you want to talk. In the meantime, you'd better be doing your sit-ups every morning or I'll kick your sorry ass when you get home. Later."

Luke didn't have to think before dialing. Aaron picked up

after a few rings.

"Aaron. Is this a bad time?"

"No, no. I just got back from my lunchtime jog. The beach is amazing today, man."

"I bet." Luke thought wistfully of home.

"So how are you doing?"

Luke barked out a sharp laugh. "I've been better. Everyone's staring at me like I've got three heads."

"To be expected, I guess."

"I guess."

"So you're denying it?"

"Of course! What else would I do?"

"Well, there's always the truth, Luke. Come on, it's the twenty-first century, right?"

Luke snorted. "You must be living in a different world than me, Aaron."

"Hey, no one said it would be easy."

"You should have seen the guys today. The way they looked at me. No way they'd ever accept a queer on the tour."

"Okay, so maybe it's too soon. What does Jesse think?"

"He agrees with me. There's no way we can come out. His career is just starting. He'd never get a major sponsor, and he's probably going to have some trouble already because of this."

"If he starts to win, though, no one can argue with that."

"No, but they can sure make his life miserable." Luke's gut twisted at the thought of what it could be like for Jesse. His whole career could be in jeopardy. At least Luke had already had his share of victories, his moments in the sun.

"But you know, a gay man's never going to be accepted on the tour if everyone stays locked in the closet."

"Well, someone else can take the heat, Aaron. I have more important things on my mind, like this damn tournament. If I win my next few matches, I'm on track to meet Koehler in the semis. And I should have these guys I'm up against beat."

"Hell, it would be great to see you knock out Koehler."

Luke's jaw set. "You have no idea. Just the other day he was needling me about Jesse, and now suddenly the press is watching our rooms and they get an incriminating photo."

"Hmm. Coincidence?"

"Possibly. But with that bastard, I'm inclined to think not."

"Son of a bitch."

"I've got to beat him." Luke felt the familiar competitive desire pumping through his veins, accompanied by a newfound rage.

"So do it. Play your best, man. You can do it."

"Thanks, Aaron." Luke cleared his throat. "You're a good friend." He and Aaron had known each other for years but didn't exactly have many deep and meaningful conversations. Probably because Luke kept most people at arm's length.

"Anytime, Luke. Anytime. Hang in there, okay?"

"Okay. Thanks. And I'm doing my sit-ups, don't worry."

"You'd better be!" Aaron laughed.

They said goodbye and Luke listened to the dial tone. He knew Jesse was home and after a moment's hesitation, dialed his number. It rang repeatedly until Jesse's voicemail picked up.

"Jess. It's me. Just wanted to make sure you got home okay." Luke sighed. He wanted to talk to him, missed him more than he thought possible. "Things here are okay, I guess. Could be worse. Hope everything's okay for you. Well, I'd better go. I miss you. Talk to you soon."

Luke hung up and winced—he always tended to ramble on answering machines. He flipped on the TV and tried to find something mindless. Anything but the news, anything but seeing his own face and hearing everyone speculate on his life, on Jesse.

The phone rang and he wished desperately that the hotel had call display. Taking the chance that it was Jesse returning his call, Luke picked up. "Hello?"

"Ross? What the hell is going on? Why haven't you returned my calls? Jesus Christ, you'd better have a good explanation. The people at Top Spin are not happy, do you hear me?" Arnie Lachance's voice boomed down the line.

"Arnie." Luke winced. He was hoping to save this conversation for another day. Preferably, after he'd beaten Koehler to reach the finals. "I was just about to call you."

"Don't shit a shitter, Luke."

"Look, this whole thing is crazy. You know how the British press is; they're the worst in the world. They'll make up anything to sell papers."

"Right. So it's not true? You and this McAllister kid?"

"Of course it's not true!" The lies came so easily to his lips.

"So why do they have a picture of you two getting it on?" Good old Arnie. As blunt as ever.

"We're not! Jesus, Arn. The kid was upset about losing; I gave him a hug that lasted for about two seconds. Of course they make it look like it's something else, something worse."

Arnie was silent for a few moments. "Okay. But if there's more to this story, you'd better tell me right now. Because Top Spin isn't going to want someone light in the loafers wearing their logo."

"There's nothing more to tell." Luke felt sick. At least Arnie was truthful. *This* was the reaction most people would have, and Luke wasn't about to jeopardize his endorsements.

"Okay, Ross. Then keep the hell away from that kid and start winning some more matches, you hear?"

"That's the plan, boss."

"All right. I have to get on the blower with Top Spin and assure them that their spokesman isn't some fucking fairy. Talk to you soon."

Luke opened his mouth to say goodbye, but Arnie was already gone. He hung up the phone and flopped back on the bed. After staring at a small, faint crack in the ceiling for a long time, Luke roused himself.

He ordered his chicken breast dinner and wished that Jesse wasn't across the ocean.

THE GRASS WAS slick under his feet and Luke struggled to maintain his balance as he changed directions quickly. He stabbed at the ball as it flew by, barely getting his racquet on it. The ball flew up and bounced harmlessly back to the court.

Across the net, Koehler pumped his fist and shouted encouragement to himself. He'd been ahead before the rain delay, and he was continuing to dominate afterwards. It was early in the third set, and after winning a tiebreak in the first set, Koehler was steamrolling over Luke.

Luke took a minute to towel his face before motioning to a ball boy for another ball to serve. It was only love-15, but Luke already felt like he was down break point. He mentally shook himself, knowing that that kind of attitude wasn't helping him. But his legs felt like lead and his shots just weren't working for him. His first-serve percentage was dipping precipitously low, giving Koehler many slower, easier-to-return second serves.

He tossed the ball up and brought his racquet around to launch it over the net. Unfortunately, like way too many of his first serves in the match, it didn't make it over. To avoid the risk of double faulting, the second serve had to be slower and safer. Predictably, Koehler pounced on it and put it away into the corner.

Love-30. The crowd cheered on Luke, but he was sure it was because most of them wanted a longer match, not because they particularly wanted him to win. However, he did have some loyal, vocal fans in the audience, as he had all week. They'd been speaking up in his defense in the media and all over the Internet, denying his homosexuality.

On one hand it was a relief, but on the other…he wasn't sure what to think.

The last week had felt very, very long. Luke had spoken to Jesse a few times, but after hearing a clicking noise on the line one day, Luke was now paranoid the phone was bugged. If a recording got out, they'd be finished. He decided it would be best to just wait until he got home to speak to Jesse again. Even his cell phone wasn't safe, not with all the modern devices to pick up other people's signals.

Jesse had seemed very far away, and Luke knew it wasn't just the miles between them. He said that everything was fine with his family, and that the press weren't bothering him too much. Mostly he changed the subject and talked about practicing with Jeff, about how his backhand volley was improving daily.

Luke tried to put it out of his mind and concentrate on the match he was playing. The match he was losing. He squared his shoulders, served again, and won the point with an ace that Koehler couldn't even touch. It was only Luke's fifth ace of the match, a very low figure for him considering it was the third set.

The crowd clapped and Luke tried to pump himself up. At least the whispers had slowed, and no one had called him any names while he was on the court. He'd gone on British TV and debunked the rumors with humor and his dashing smile, and the public seemed to be buying it. Alex had done him a favor and given an interview to the biggest newspaper in London, telling them all about how Luke had been a passionate lover and she was sure he wasn't gay.

One night he had seen Jesse on the news, microphones shoved in his face as he headed into Brookview to practice. He had looked very young and very nervous. Luke had cringed at the fear he saw in Jesse's eyes, because he knew others would see it, too. Jesse had refused to comment.

Thankfully, there was also a new scandal in the headlines: Regina O'Brien, a young and beautiful American player, had been caught red-handed with one of England's hottest actors. Said actor also happened to be married with children, and the press was having a field day.

Luke served at 15-30 and missed. He tried to put some extra juice on his second serve, and double faulted. He cursed under his breath and took his time before serving at 15-40. Looking across the net at Koehler, Luke wanted to throw down his racquet and leap over there to pummel the bastard's smarmy face. Koehler was really enjoying this.

Instead, he served and they rallied back and forth and just when Luke thought he'd won the point, Koehler dug deep and made a cross-court backhand that was just out of Luke's reach.

Just like most things were these days.

"AND STEIN BREAKS again to go up five-three. Looks like he'll be serving the match out in the next game."

Steve Anderson sighed. The final would be between the German and the Russian, which wouldn't be great for ratings in the States. But that was life. He'd still get his paycheck either way.

As the players switched sides, Steve ruminated on Luke's woes. "It's been a tough tournament for Rossovich, dealing with all the rumors and speculation about his personal life. That's always hard on a player, especially when the gossip is so nasty. But Ross's fans have supported him and I'm sure he'll put this behind him very soon."

Koehler started serving for the match, quickly going up 30-love on the strength of two aces. "Well, it looks like Luke Rossovich isn't going to get to another Wimbledon final. He might be back next year, but he'll be thirty-five by then, and I'm just not sure his body can take another year on the tour. Still, he's a great champion and he has the U.S. Open coming up. He's never won there, and he wants it badly before his career ends."

Koehler finished out the match and jogged to the net to meet Luke. They smiled at each other and shook hands good-naturedly. "Ross is always a gracious loser, and I know he and Stein have a lot of respect for each other. It's always great to see two class acts on the court."

As they went to commercial, Steve looked over at his fellow commentator. "I'll bet you a hundred bucks Rossovich punches Koehler in the locker room."

STEIN KOEHLER'S SHIRT bunched in Luke's fists as he slammed the German against the bank of lockers. Koehler had made one too many sneering digs at Luke, and a man could only put up with so much.

"Hey, hey!" Koehler's coach rounded the corner and shouted out. "Get off him, Rossovich!"

A small crowd gathered and with a great deal of willpower, Luke took a step back, releasing Koehler from his grasp.

"Luke, I know it must be hard to keep your hands off me, but do try to resist." Koehler smiled as he straightened his shirt. He reminded Luke of a wolf about to devour its prey.

"Just stay the hell out of my way," Luke gritted out. "And I'll stay out of yours."

"Don't worry; I'm too busy thinking about winning my next Wimbledon to bother with you." Koehler smiled again, and it was everything Luke could do to keep his fists at his side.

"Well, I'm still one up on you; this will only be your second if you can manage to take down Tikohnov."

"Ah, but I'm only twenty-six, Luke. I still have my best years ahead of me. You, on the other hand ..." Koehler let his silence speak for itself.

Luke opened his mouth to retort when Mike arrived and pulled him away quickly and bustled him out of the room. "Come on; don't let that asshole bother you. He's not worth it, buddy."

In the hall, Luke took several deep breaths. "I know, you're right."

"What was he saying? He's always the worst winner."

"You know it." Luke shook his head and tried to laugh. "It was just the usual taunts and snickering." He didn't mention the comments about Jesse, the innuendo and sly glances. Luke was more sure than ever that Koehler had tipped off the photographer who'd taken the compromising picture.

Which made losing to him even harder to swallow. Luke vowed it wouldn't happen again.

HIS FLIGHT HOME was long, and Luke still felt like everyone was watching him out of the corner of their eye. A few times he caught a woman across the aisle staring, until she finally kept her eyes on her book. Luke had a few drinks and eventually drifted off to sleep somewhere over the Atlantic.

He was only home ten minutes when the bell rang. He shut the door quickly behind Jesse and pulled him close—breathing him in, reveling in the feel of him, solid once more in his arms.

"It's so good to see you again," Luke murmured.

"You, too."

"I missed you."

Jesse leaned back and kissed Luke tenderly. "I missed you, too." His fingers grazed Luke's cheek and then he took a step backwards, squaring his shoulders.

"What's wrong?"

"Luke …"

"No one followed you, did they? I hired security to stay at the end of the driveway to keep the press away. It should be fine."

Jesse walked into the living room and shook his head. "No, no one followed me."

"What is it?" He sounded…defeated, and it was putting Luke on edge. He reached out for him, but Jesse backed up a step.

"I can't believe I'm going to say this, but…somehow I am."

"What? Jesse, what's going on?" Luke's heart began thumping in his chest.

"I can't do this. I can't live a lie."

"What? You're upset, I understand."

"No! I don't think you do." Jesse took a shuddering breath, blowing it out slowly. "I came home from London and talked to my parents. I told them that there was nothing going on, that it was a misunderstanding, that I wasn't gay. Luke, I lied to their faces."

"It's just the way it has to be for now. I know it's hard." Luke tried to take his hand, but Jesse moved out of reach.

"You should have seen my father's expression. I can't get it out of my mind. He was so disappointed. He can barely look at me anymore; he knows I'm lying. My mother knows. They all *know*, Luke. I think they always have. They were just waiting for me to say something."

"Okay, so tell your family the truth. You're right, they deserve to know." Luke thought of his own mother, of her acceptance. "And you deserve it, too. I was wrong."

"I am going to tell them. Tonight."

"Okay. You're right, you should. I was being selfish. I'm sorry." He tried once more to draw Jesse near.

"I'm sorry, too." Jesse's eyes glistened and he kept Luke at arm's length. "I can't do this anymore. I can't sneak around and pretend that I'm someone I'm not. Now that everyone suspects, we'll never have a moment's peace, wondering who's listening or watching or taking pictures. I can't live like that."

"Jesse, you're upset. It'll be fine." Luke's heart was hammering in his chest and fear chilled his veins. "It'll be okay."

"No, it won't. I can't be with you if we're not going to be honest."

"Honest?" Luke snapped. "Can you imagine what it would be like on the tour if the guys knew the truth? What it would be like in the locker room? All we'd get for our honesty is grief."

"Maybe. But someone has to be the first; someone has to have the balls."

"What, so you can do the talk show circuit and write a moving autobiography on being the first openly gay male tennis player? I'm sure Oprah will lap it up. Is that what this is about? Getting attention?"

"No!" Jesse moved even further away, incredulity on his face. "I can't believe you'd think that. This is about being honest. About being *me*. It took a long time to figure out just who that was. I can't sneak around, always looking over my shoulder. Always waiting for the other shoe to drop."

"So, what, it's over? Just like that?" Luke's stomach roiled. He wanted to pinch himself and wake up. This had to be a nightmare.

"Unless you can come clean. Come out. People may surprise you, Luke. Maybe it won't be that bad." Jesse reached out his hand, but it was Luke's turn to back away.

"It will be. In case you haven't noticed, anti-gay sentiment is running pretty high in this country. Not to mention other places in the world. I couldn't even go to some tournaments because I'd be afraid for my life."

"But there are plenty of lesbians on the women's tour, and they're fine."

"It's not the same. It's just not, and you know it."

"Okay, it's not. But it doesn't mean it can't change."

"Well, I'm not going to be the guinea pig, Jesse. I'm thirty-four fucking years old. My career is almost over. Hell, this could be it for me on tour after this year. I need to concentrate on winning, not on being a poster boy for gay rights groups."

"I know. I understand. I do. I won't say anything publicly right now, not until you've retired. Just 'no comment,' I guess. Only because I know what it'll do to you."

Luke huffed in frustration. "So then it's fine, we can still see each other."

"No, Luke. We can't. I can't sneak around and pretend that I'm not seeing you. That I don't love you." Tears threatened to spill from Jesse's eyes and Luke longed to take him into his arms.

"Jess...what are you...so that's it? It's over?"

Sniffing, Jesse shrugged sadly. "Yeah, I guess it is. I don't feel like I have any choice."

Luke barked out a laugh, sharp-edged. "You have a choice. And you're making it. I guess I'm not important enough to you."

"Is that what you really think? I love you, Luke. I want to be with you. But not like this. Don't you see? We deserve more." Jesse cried, tears flowing freely. "Aren't you sick of all the lies?"

"I didn't make the rules! We live in a world that doesn't accept us! I'm just doing what I have to do to get by, to be a success."

"Luke, you're a champion. No one can ever take that away from you!"

"You think I'd have six-figure endorsements if everyone knew I was queer? That's not how the world works! Stop being so fucking naïve."

"I'm not." Jesse clenched his jaw and wiped away the rest of his tears. "I'm just not misanthropic like you are. The world's changing, Luke. I'm not saying it would be easy, but not everyone hates us. Not by a long shot."

"You're young," Luke scoffed. "You think you can change the

world. You'll see. You have to look out for yourself."

"You're right. I do." He took a deep breath and walked to the front door. He stopped, his hand on the knob. His shoulders shook and he whispered, "I'm going miss you so much."

Luke wanted to haul him back, refuse to let him go. The thought of living without him was terrifying and nausea coursed through his body, almost brought him to his knees.

But he said nothing.

"See ya." Jesse left without looking back.

Luke's legs wavered and he grabbed the wall for support. He slid down slowly, leaning back. The setting sun cast long shadows, and soon darkness settled in. Luke watched the patterns on the wall, the trees outside dappling the moonlight. He concentrated on breathing, the hollow feeling in his chest making every inhalation a struggle.

CHAPTER FOURTEEN

★★★ ★★★

THE NEXT FEW weeks dragged by unbearably. Every day Luke fought the urge to call Jesse, to try to talk him around. Jesse was being crazy, thinking that he could just come out and be welcomed with open arms. Life wasn't like that, certainly not as a male professional athlete.

Luke worked out with Aaron and steadfastly refused to discuss the situation with him. Eventually, Aaron stopped bringing it up and they worked out mostly in silence. Luke's mother had tried to talk to him about Jesse, too, but gave up.

They just didn't understand.

Everyone down at the club assured him they didn't believe the ridiculous gossip, but Luke saw the way they looked at him, the way conversations would stop when he walked by. Most importantly, Mike hadn't been able—or willing—to practice with him in a week. At first it was a missed session here and there, but now as the days passed and Mike didn't call, Luke knew something was up. He should never have told Mike the truth. No matter how open-minded most people thought they were, reality often told a different story.

Some would call him paranoid, but Luke preferred to think of it as being practical. He understood the way the world worked, even if others wanted to believe differently. Thankfully, the press had stopped coming around and had moved on to the next celebrity scandal they could exploit. Luke was glad to be able to answer the phone again.

Of course, every time it rang he hoped it was Jesse.

As Luke pulled into his driveway one night, his headlights illuminated his mother's red Honda. She wasn't inside, so for once she must have used her key. Luke sighed. He should have been happy to see his mother, but he was afraid he was in for another lecture.

"Mom?" He closed the front door behind him and dropped his tennis gear at the foot of the stairs.

He heard the TV in the other room and found his mother on the couch. She muted the television, which was playing footage of one of Luke's old matches.

"Hello, sweetheart." Stephanie smiled up at him and Luke dropped a kiss on her cheek as he joined her on the couch.

"Don't you have all these matches on tape at home?"

"Yes, but I haven't watched any of them in ages."

"What, you mean you don't relive my greatest moments on a nightly basis? What kind of mother are you?" Luke teased.

"The kind with a life of her own who didn't obsessively travel with you to every tournament when you were younger."

"Thank god for that," Luke said, shuddering. Tennis parents were notorious on the tour, often coaching and controlling every aspect of their child's life—on and off the court. The problem was worse on the women's side, but the men's tour had its share of overbearing families.

They watched Luke playing on the screen in silence for a few moments. It was his Australian Open victory.

"I was always sorry I wasn't there to see you win, Luke."

He shrugged. "You had work, and it was halfway around the world. I understood."

"Still, sometimes I think back on my life and ..." She trailed off.

"And what?"

"Oh, don't mind me." She waved her hand and smiled. "I'm just feeling old and maudlin today."

"No, tell me."

She looked at him and Luke could see the sadness in her eyes. He knew she missed his father. She'd never remarried and as far as Luke knew, she didn't date. She tucked a lock of brown hair behind her ear. "Sometimes I think back on things I didn't do because I was too busy, or too tired, or too whatever. Too scared, sometimes. And when you get older, you realize that life only gives you so many opportunities."

"Mom, you're talking like you've got one foot in the grave." Suddenly his heart skipped a beat. "You're not...you're not sick?"

She laughed genuinely. "No, no. Nothing like that. Just a bit melancholy."

"You're sure?"

"Yes, I'm sure." She patted his hand. "You always were a worrier, even when you were a little boy. And you still are."

He shrugged. "I guess."

Onscreen, the camera cut to Nik in the crowd, on his feet, clapping for Luke as he took the second set. Watching him, Luke suddenly felt a wave of loneliness. Nik had been gone for so long now, and Luke didn't think he'd ever be able to think of him without feeling a tug of emotion. However, it was the past.

Now he longed for Jesse. For the present, for the future that could have been. Jesse was so close, but out of reach.

"What do you think Nik would say if he were here?"

Luke jolted out of his thoughts. "What?"

"Do you think he'd like to see you so unhappy? Hiding from the world?"

"He would understand, Mom. He always did. He knew we had to keep our relationship a secret. He agreed with me." Luke jumped to his feet and clicked the TV off. "Is that why you're here? To give me a guilt trip?"

"Honey, I'm here because I don't want you to make the biggest mistake of your life."

"What's that, exactly?"

Stephanie sighed and got to her feet. "I understand why you're afraid. Nevertheless, I think Jesse's right. It's time to be honest—with yourself, with your friends, with everyone. Living your life in secret, always looking over your shoulder waiting for disaster…that's no way to live."

"And how exactly do you know what Jesse thinks? I don't remember discussing it with you."

"No, you didn't. So I discussed it with him myself."

"You what?" Luke fumed. "How dare you go behind my back."

"You didn't leave me much choice. I tried to get you to open up, to listen to other points of view, but you're stubborn to the end, Luke. So I went to see him. He really is a lovely young man, you know."

"Thanks for the memo, Mom. I don't need you to tell me anything about Jesse."

"Well, maybe you do! He loves you, and I think he's hoping that you'll come to your senses and see that there *is* another way. The only one keeping you in the closet is *you*."

"Right," Luke spat. "There's no more homophobia in the world and if I come out, the world will just accept me with open arms while they wave little rainbow flags. With hearts on them."

"I know you're angry. I know that the world isn't a perfect place. However, are you really willing to give up the person who made you happy for the first time in years? Just because you're afraid of what others might think?"

"I told Mike, and now I barely see him. He said it didn't change anything, but it does, Mom. It does."

"Maybe he just needs time to adjust. You have to be patient."

"Mom, it's more than just that." Luke ran his hand through his hair. Why couldn't she understand? "It's about my livelihood. The only endorsements I'd have if I came out would be for gay products. I'd be that gay tennis player. I'd lose a hell of a lot of money."

"You've already made more than enough money. Yes, you're right; you would be the gay tennis player." She moved forward a step and took his hand between her own. "But you'd be the gay tennis player who won four Grand Slams—and maybe more, your career isn't quite over yet. You'd still be a champion, Luke."

"Yeah, and what about Jesse? He's just getting started, and I won't be around to …" He shook his head. "Forget it."

"To protect him? Maybe he doesn't need your protection, Luke. Maybe all he wants is to live his life in the open. With you."

"You make it sound so easy." He let her hold his hand, even though he wanted to pull away.

"No, it isn't easy. Not many things in life are. Not the things that matter, anyway. Is it easy to lose Jesse?"

Luke swallowed, his throat suddenly dry. "No."

"Then just think about what I've said. All right?"

He nodded and she pulled him into her arms. He stood stiffly at first, then gave in, lowering his head to her shoulder and letting her murmur comfort as she rubbed his back. He closed his eyes and breathed in her perfume.

THE NEXT TOURNAMENT Luke was playing was in LA., much to his relief. He could go home at night and not have to sleep in yet another in the endless line of hotel rooms.

Luke had barely pushed the locker room door open when he heard the word "faggot" and raucous laughter.

Great.

As the door closed behind him, he realized that he wasn't the object of their scorn. Jesse was by a bench, his head down as he tied his shoes and ignored the taunts coming from the other players in the room.

Stein Koehler came around the corner from the shower, a towel slung around his hips. He gazed at Jesse scornfully. "I'm amazed you can hold up your racquet with such a limp wrist."

There was a chorus of laughter from some of the others, including the Stiffler brothers, to Luke's dismay. Anger roared through him and the next thing Luke knew, he had Koehler slammed up against the wall.

Their faces were inches apart and Luke practically growled, "Watch your mouth, you son of a bitch." He itched to wipe the smile off the bastard's face.

Snickering, Koehler said, "Finally got me where you want me, Luke?"

Luke swore and backed away. The day he'd want to touch that piece of shit was never coming.

Koehler adjusted his towel and made a theatrical sigh. "Jesse, your boyfriend just can't keep his hands off me. How jealous you must be."

Closing his locker, Jesse smiled. "Painfully jealous, Stein. I just don't know what I shall do." He walked out, his laughter trailing in his wake. Some of the players looked around at each other in uncertainty.

Luke shook his head and tried to follow Jesse's lead. He laughed and ignored Koehler and his cronies. Mike came in and stopped short when he saw Luke. "Hey. How's it going?"

Luke swallowed the retort he wanted to make. "Fine. Is Tara feeling better?"

"Huh?"

"Tara. You said she's been sick the past couple of weeks."

He could see the blush creep up Mike's neck. "Oh, right. She's much better now, thanks."

"Want to go hit some shots?" Luke's heart was in his throat as he waited for Mike's answer. *Please say yes.*

He smiled. "Sure thing."

AFTER PRACTICE WITH Mike, who was quiet and didn't bring up anything more controversial than the weather, Luke played his first match. It was an easy victory, claimed just as the sun started to set. The smog was thick and Luke could see it clearly in the distance, high over the city as the sun started its downward arc.

He packed up his gear and headed back inside. It was late, and the building was pretty deserted. He was almost to the locker room when he heard his name hissed from a doorway.

Jesse stuck his head out. "Get in here," he said, backing up into an empty, windowless office. Luke complied, shutting the door behind him.

"What the hell was that?" Jesse demanded.

"What?"

"Your little performance in the locker room," he seethed.

"You can't let that asshole Koehler talk to you like that! I was standing up for you." Luke dropped his bag with a thunk and his hands found his hips.

"By acting like an overprotective boyfriend?" Jesse was incredulous. "Yeah, that'll really diffuse those rumors, Luke."

"What was I supposed to do? Nothing?"

"Yes. Nothing. Laugh it off. Ignore it. But when you let people like that get under your skin, you're just giving them new stuff to gossip about."

Luke knew he was right, but he didn't want to admit it. "Well, excuse me for standing up for you."

Rubbing his face, Jesse sighed. "Luke, this is your secret. I'm keeping it for *your* sake. If it was just me they were calling queer, I'd get up on a table and announce to everyone that they were right. Because eventually, they'd get over it."

"Maybe. But in the meantime, your life would be hell."

"Yeah, probably. At least it would all be out there. There'd be no more bullshit."

"Jesse…"

"I know, I know. Look, I'm not trying to convince you. That's obviously a lost cause. You do what you need to do." He tried to smile, and Luke hated the sadness he saw. "But just try to think twice before you get into fights with jerks like Stein Koehler."

"You're right." They stood in silence for a few seconds, eyes locked. "I just hate the thought of anyone hurting you." Luke took a step and ran his fingers over Jesse's cheek. He could see Jesse fighting himself, fighting the urge to draw closer. All at once, he moved into Luke's arms, warm and pliant.

They stood entwined for a long time, just breathing each other in, arms wrapped tightly. "Luke," Jesse murmured.

They kissed, tongues winding together, lips soft. Luke's hands moved under Jesse's shirt, caressing him. When Jesse gasped for breath, Luke's lips moved to his neck, sucking the tender skin into his mouth, leaving his mark. He slipped his hand into Jesse's shorts, grasping his hardening cock.

Suddenly Jesse wrenched away, breathing hard.

"Jess …" Luke reached out for him again.

"No," he said, backing away. "I can't. Nothing's changed, Luke. Look at us. Hiding away in a dark room, sneaking around to even talk to each other."

"It doesn't have to be like this all the time." Luke's body thrummed with desire and he ached to have Jesse in his arms once more.

Shaking his head sadly, Jesse said, "But it is." He hurried out of the room, the door banging shut in his wake.

Luke slumped back against the wall, defeated.

CHAPTER FIFTEEN

THE REST OF the tournament was a blur. Luke got to the final and won handily against a young Swiss player everyone was touting as the next big thing. Luke didn't realize until the mandatory press conference afterwards that it was his first title of the season.

When the reporters asked about the controversy at Wimbledon, Luke took Jesse's advice and laughed it off. He made a few jokes that had everyone tittering, and afterwards one of the female reporters approached him and slipped her number in his pocket.

It shocked him a bit that he hadn't won more tournaments, and that he hadn't even *noticed* he wasn't winning. He'd been so preoccupied with Jesse, nothing much else had registered. Luke vowed to capitalize on his victory and try to keep some momentum going into the upcoming U.S. Open.

When Luke arrived at Brookview, he was glad to see that Amber wasn't behind the receptionist's desk. She was a nice girl, but he wasn't in the mood to be charming.

Mike was mysteriously busy again, so Luke was meeting another old friend from the tour, Andy Dohring, for some hitting. Andy played out of Brookview, and Luke just hoped that he wouldn't run into Jesse. It was late in the day, and he knew Jesse was an early riser. Luke could only hope that Jesse and Jeff had already put in a full day's work and left.

As he headed towards the court Andy had reserved, Luke immediately saw that it wasn't his lucky day. Jesse was a few courts over, practicing his groundstrokes while Jeff shouted instructions from the sideline.

As Luke passed by, he tried to remain unnoticed. Jeff paused in mid-diatribe when he saw him, but quickly regained his train of thought. However, Jesse noticed that Jeff's attention wandered and glanced over his shoulder as Luke walked by.

Their eyes met and Luke felt a jolt as he ground to a halt. He missed Jesse so much. He longed to just sweep him up into his arms and never let go.

Jesse finally blinked and determinedly pivoted back around. Luke forced his legs into action and made his way to his court, where Andy waited. Andy was a journeyman like Mike who'd never win the big tournaments. He was affable and talkative and Luke was happy to let him take the lead and blather on until they took their sides of the court.

After a long hitting session, they called it a night. Luke had tried to keep his attention where it belonged, but his eyes had inevitably drifted over to Jesse occasionally in between points. For his part, Jesse seemed totally focused, listening to Jeff's coaching and keeping his eye on the ball.

When Luke walked by again on his way out, Jesse didn't look over. He tried not to care but failed miserably.

In the parking lot, he said goodnight to Andy and headed to his SUV. Once inside, he just sat with his hands on the wheel, the key not even in the ignition. Darkness was falling, but there was some kind of party going on in the country club restaurant, so the lot was still almost full.

Jeff and Jesse walked out some time later, and Luke watched as Jeff slapped him on the back and headed to his car. Jesse headed the other way, towards Luke. Luke's heart sped up as he watched Jesse go to his little hatchback a few rows away.

Before Luke could even think about it, he was dialing Jesse's cell phone. Through the windshield, he could see him under the lights of the parking lot at his car door. Jesse pulled his cell from his pocket and stared at the display as the phone rang in Luke's ear.

Finally, just before it went to voicemail, Jesse picked up. "Hey."

"Hey." Luke couldn't think of a single thing to say.

"So. What's up?"

"Nothing, I just wanted to…I don't know." Hear his voice. Connect.

"Um, okay. How's it going?"

"It's fine. You know, getting ready for the Open." Luke felt ridiculous. "Look, it's late, I won't keep you."

"No, wait!" Jesse cleared his throat. "It's good to talk to you. It's weird how I see you, but it's as if you might as well be a million miles away. You know?"

Luke knew just what he meant. "It was your choice, Jesse. Anytime you want to see reason, I'll be here."

Jesse squared his shoulders and the warmth was gone from his voice. "Right. Forget I said anything."

God, he looked beautiful when he was determined.

"What?"

"What?" Luke suddenly had the sinking sensation that he'd spoken his thought aloud.

"You said…you said I looked…" Jesse glanced around, his eyes flicking over all the vehicles. "Are you watching me?" He didn't seem to notice Luke's black SUV, but it wasn't surprising since there were so many in the lot.

"Yeah, I'm watching you."

"Where are you?" Jesse was still looking.

"Around."

"Oh, so you're stalking me now?" Jesse half laughed.

"Maybe I am," Luke teased. "And you look hot when you're half scared."

"Oh, shut the hell up!" He was fully laughing now, and Luke loved the sound.

"You really do look hot. Good enough to eat."

He could hear Jesse swallow hard. "Stop it. I'm hanging up."

"I would strip you down and bend you over the hood of that car, and the metal would be hot against your bare skin, after being in the sun all day. But my tongue in your ass would be even hotter. I'd eat you until your cock was hard and leaking."

Jesse leaned against the car door and took a shuddering breath. "What else would you do?" he whispered.

"I'd turn you over and spread your legs wide, suck your cock while my fingers played in your hole." As he spoke, Luke stroked himself through his jeans. "I'd make you beg me to fuck you."

Jesse was breathing hard and then he was out of sight, the car door closing behind him. "I would, you know. Beg you."

Luke bit back a groan and unzipped his pants, his hand stroking his hot, hard flesh. "You want me to pound your tight little ass?"

"Yes. God, yes."

"Can you feel me? I'm inside you, and the heat is almost too much. It's just skin on skin."

"Yes, I feel you," Jesse panted.

"Your legs are up on my shoulders and you're wide open for me." Luke closed his eyes, imagining it in his mind.

"Fuck me. Fuck me harder."

Luke's hand moved rapidly on his cock and he knew Jesse did the same. "I'm going to come inside you; I'm going to spill in your hot ass."

"Do it, Luke. Fuck me, come inside me, don't ever leave." Then with a strangled cry, he came.

At the sound of Jesse's orgasm, Luke's balls tightened and he tugged once more before he spurted on his hand. He milked himself, and both he and Jesse tried to catch their breath.

"I miss you so much," Jesse muttered.

Luke swallowed, hard. "I miss you, too." When Jesse didn't say anything, he added, "It doesn't have to be like this. Come back to my place. Let me do all those things for real."

It sounded like Jesse whimpered, but Luke couldn't be sure. "And tomorrow?"

"Let's not worry about tomorrow. Not now."

"I wish it was that easy. God, I wish it was. But tomorrow will come, Luke. And we'll still be in the same place we are now."

"We don't have to be. If you'd just be reasonable—"

"*Reasonable*? I've been very reasonable."

Luke's jaw set. "No, you've been very young. Very naïve."

"Fuck you. Don't treat me as if I'm some stupid kid who doesn't know what he's doing. Who doesn't know what he wants. Because I do."

"What you want is a dream world that doesn't exist!"

For a few moments, Luke could hear Jesse's uneven breathing. Then the dial tone resonated in his ear and he watched Jesse peel out of the parking lot. Luke closed his eyes and leaned his head back. He wanted to follow but knew he couldn't.

TORONTO WAS HOT and muggy, a preview of what New York would undoubtedly be like during the U.S. Open. When Luke arrived at the tennis center, he looked at the draw for the tournament, which was posted on a big board. He noted that Jesse's name wasn't listed. Jesse had played the week before at a tournament in Washington, and Luke knew it was to avoid him.

He should have been relieved, but he wasn't. He hadn't seen Jesse in a couple of weeks and now he wouldn't see him again until the end of the month when the tennis world descended on New York City.

Mike had gotten through qualifying and the first round. When Luke saw him in the locker room, he tried to act normal. "Good match today." His voice was a strange pitch and he winced.

"Hey, buddy. Thanks." Mike still seemed awkward, and Luke realized that things probably would never go back to the way they used to be. He missed his friend.

"Guess I'll see you around." Luke shut his locker and was gone.

Luke's first two matches were a breeze and he spent some time playing tennis with local kids and doing some publicity events around the city. He played a short match with another player on a court set up at the foot of the CN Tower. A huge crowd gathered, as the Blue Jays were playing at the dome next door.

Luke signed hundreds of autographs, his hand sore by the time he was whisked away to watch the baseball game in a special box. Waitresses served canapés and martinis, and one flirted shamelessly with Luke. She was small and blonde and all he could think of was Jesse. He hobnobbed with the Tennis Canada bigwigs and played his part, smiling and joking and being an ambassador for the sport.

It was exhausting sometimes.

The tournament rolled on, and Luke made the semis in relatively easy fashion. Then he came up against Stein Koehler once again. The sneering German still made innuendo-laced comments to Luke whenever he saw him, but Luke was determined to ignore it.

He was also determined to beat him. He flew Aaron up to Toronto so he'd have a friend in the stands and toyed with the idea of asking his mother to come. But she had her own life, her own business. She couldn't just leave the flower store at the drop of a hat.

Unfortunately, the match didn't go Luke's way. In fact, it was a disaster. Luke just couldn't seem to find his groove and Koehler took him in straight sets, 6-4, 6-3. When they shook hands at the net, Luke forced a smile onto his face and uttered a few meaningless words of congratulations.

Luke showered quickly and dutifully put in his appearance at the press conference afterwards. He answered questions with the standard doublespeak athletes use, talking about giving a hundred and ten percent and getting his legs under him and in the end, not really saying much of anything at all. However, he did vow to be in top form at the U.S. Open in two weeks.

That night in Luke's hotel room, Aaron sipped a light beer and looked out at the city's high rises in the distance.

"Your training couldn't be better; you're in the best shape possible. It's your mental game that's not up to snuff, Luke."

Sitting back against the headboard, Luke swallowed some of his own beer. "Maybe. On the other hand, maybe that bastard is just impossible to beat. He's been number one all year for a reason."

"No one's impossible to beat. You just need to keep focused and find his weak spot."

Luke snorted. "Well, he's certainly found mine. I can't prove it, but I know he tipped off the press in London."

"You need to just forget about that. Focus on your game."

"Easy for you to say. If it wasn't for that son of a bitch, Jesse would be here right now."

"Well, pardon me."

Luke smiled. "Sorry. You know what I mean."

Aaron flopped down on the bed. "Yeah, I know. But you know, I'm not sure things would be so different."

"What are you talking about?" Luke peered down at Aaron beside him. Of course things would be different.

"Maybe it wouldn't have happened so fast, but it would have happened. Jesse would have gotten tired of hiding eventually."

"You don't know that."

Aaron took a long look at Luke and said, "Yeah, I do. And I can't blame him."

"Oh, so you're taking his side?" Luke slammed his beer down on the side table.

"It's not about sides."

"You're supposed to be my friend." Luke knew he sounded like a twelve-year-old, but he couldn't stop himself.

Sitting up, Aaron shook his head. "I *am* your friend. That's why I'm saying this. Because someone has to. You're so stuck in the closet that you can't see how it affects the people around you."

"Well, do enlighten me."

"You won't even admit to people that *I'm* gay, and I've been out of the closet since I was sixteen! I'm a personal trainer. In *LA*. The only people who really believe I'm straight are…well, actually, I'm not sure there is anyone."

"So what, does it kill you to not be waving a rainbow pride flag around when you're with me?"

He sighed. "I play along when I'm with you because you pay me a hell of a lot of money, and because you're my friend. But if I were Jesse, I would have done the same thing. It's too tiring to pretend to be someone you're not all the time."

Luke sprang up off the bed and paced the room. "You think I don't know that? It's the way it has to be. They'll never accept a queer on the men's tour. Hiding who we are is just as much for Jesse's sake as it is mine. His whole career is ahead of him!"

"Never is an awfully long time. Hell, it's the twenty-first century, and until someone has the balls to come out on tour and be gay and be proud, things won't change."

"It's no one's business, Aaron! What I do in my personal time is my concern."

"It's not about what you do in your spare time. It's not about who you sleep with."

"Oh, bullshit! Have you read a tabloid lately? That's all anyone cares about when you're a celebrity."

"Okay, you're right. That *is* what the public's concerned about. Gossip, rumors, anything juicy. But what about you?"

"What *about* me?"

"Maybe you're right, and to other people, being gay is about who you sleep with and that's all."

"Yes, we've established that."

"But it shouldn't be about other people."

"Well, welcome to the real world."

Aaron drained his beer and stood up, placing his hands on Luke's shoulders. "It's about who you are. And you know it." He left, the door closing quietly behind him.

Luke paced the room, returning repeatedly to stare out the window. Finally, he turned on the TV, trying to drown out the little voice in his head telling him that Aaron was right.

When that didn't work, he headed downstairs to the bar.

THE HOTEL LOBBY was quiet. As Luke waited for the elevator, he could hear nothing more than the murmurs from the reception staff over the hushed muzak. Once on board, Luke pressed the button for his floor and leaned back, his eyes drifting shut. He'd drunk more than his fair share and he felt a warm buzz through his veins.

As the elevator began moving upwards, a beep sounded quietly at each floor.

"Having a good night?"

Luke's eyes popped open and he found Jesse looking back at him. "What are you doing here?"

Jesse shrugged. "I was in the neighborhood."

"You were?" Luke shook his head, tried to clear the fog.

"Yeah. Last minute thing." A smile tugged at Jesse's lips and Luke felt a rush of blood to his cock.

Another beep and they were almost at Luke's floor. Jesse was so close, only a foot away. All Luke would have to do was reach out and he could feel him again, taste his skin, his mouth, smell him, let him fill his senses …

With a jolt of impulse, Luke jabbed the red emergency button on the elevator. It jerked to a stop somewhere between the twenty-first and twenty-second floors.

"Luke, what are you—"

Jesse's sentence cut off as Luke thrust his tongue into his mouth. He slammed Jesse up against the wall and kissed him until they were both gasping for air. Luke's fingers were tight in Jesse's hair, keeping his head in place, his mouth and throat vulnerable to Luke's kisses.

Sinking to his knees, Luke yanked Jesse's pants and underwear down to his knees, swallowing Jesse's throbbing cock deeply. His head bobbed up and down, lips and tongue working Jesse, making him groan loudly in pleasure. He inhaled deeply, Jesse's musky scent filling his nose.

When he knew Jesse was about to come, Luke pulled away and got to his feet as he turned him to face the wall. Two swift movements, and he was ramming into Jesse's ass.

It felt like paradise.

Jesse was hot and tight and he squeezed around Luke's cock, taking in every inch of him. "Harder, Luke. Harder," he muttered.

Luke's fingers bruised Jesse's hips as he thrust in and out, his balls slapping against Jesse's firm, round ass. Jesse's head tipped backwards and he moaned, his mouth open, eyes closed. Luke's teeth found his neck as he plowed into him.

When Jesse came, he shouted Luke's name and Luke felt him

shuddering around him. He pumped his hips, the wave of pleasure building before he crashed over the top, filling up Jesse with long spurts of come.

They both sank to the floor, exhausted, struggling for breath. Jesse twisted around and kissed Luke, his tongue sweeping into Luke's mouth. His blue eyes sparkled and he said something, but Luke couldn't hear it. Luke leaned in closer, but even though Jesse's lips moved again, he could hear no sound.

Suddenly Jesse began to disintegrate in Luke's arms, his body slipping away. Jesse was falling and Luke screamed, hands grasping at the air, unable to catch him as he disappeared from sight, the elevator walls gone, only blackness remaining.

Luke woke with a start, heart pounding, and reached out in the bed, searching. They had only been together a few months, but Jesse's presence had become so familiar. So comforting. Luke remembered with a sickening feeling that Jesse wasn't there.

His stomach was sticky with drying semen, but Luke couldn't be bothered to move. The memory of seeing Jesse fall was fresh in his mind and Luke worked to banish the thought. Eventually he drifted back into an uneasy sleep, waking often from disquieting dreams.

MANHATTAN WAS CROWDED and stiflingly hot, but Luke was able to walk around unnoticed and unrecognized, a baseball cap and sunglasses working wonders. He found that in New York City, as long as you stayed out of people's way, they didn't pay you much attention. Which was fine by him.

Luke wandered through Central Park, the horse-drawn carriages ferrying canoodling couples passing by every so often. He found himself by the zoo and idly watched the animals, most of whom were sleeping in the shade, much to the displeasure of the children trying to rouse them into activity.

He left the park and continued walking south, eventually finding himself in the Village as evening descended. It was Saturday night and the streets were bustling. He walked by countless restaurants with tiny patios that crowded the sidewalk, just feet from the bags of garbage that piled up endlessly in the city. Sweat dripped down the small of his back and wet the band of his cap.

The funky lamps that lit Washington Square Park buzzed with insects as he passed. NYU students and a wide variety of other people lounged about—talking, walking dogs, playing cards. A trio of men with a guitar sang Spanish melodies that he couldn't understand but liked the sound of anyway.

He stopped by the chess tables, which sat underneath signs advising against any sort of betting. Luke grinned as he noticed money changing hands near one table. Although for all he knew, it was a drug deal.

The U.S. Open was the last Grand Slam of the season, starting the week before Labor Day and continuing for two weeks, the last gasp of summer. As usual, the humidity in the city was overpowering, day and night. As Luke waited for the 7 train back to Flushing, sweat dripped down his face and his shirt stuck to him. The subway platform was a good ten degrees hotter than the street above and felt like an oven.

Rats scurried back and forth on the track, and a busker played a guitar and sang about lost love. Luke wished he didn't understand the lyrics and wandered farther down the platform, away from the music, regretting his decision not to take a cab. He didn't need the reminder of what he'd lost. He'd never told Jesse and hadn't really admitted it to himself, but if Luke was being honest, he knew the truth.

He knew he loved Jesse.

The train arrived and the doors opened with a blast of frigid air that felt like heaven. Luke chose a seat and pulled his cap a little lower on his head. He wasn't in the mood for any giggling schoolgirls to ask for his autograph. He had to rest up for his first-round match, playing whoever had gotten through qualifying in his portion of the draw. The lower-ranked players weren't automatically able to play in the tournament and had to compete in qualifying rounds first.

As the train rattled its way towards Queens, Luke's mind inevitably returned to the subject he'd been trying to avoid. He couldn't stop thinking of Jesse, couldn't stop missing him. He'd spent the morning at the Met trying to lose himself in art and history, but it was no use. It seemed like everything these days made him think of Jesse.

He sometimes pulled up Jesse's number on his cell phone, looked at the digits and ran his finger over the call button. But he never pushed it.

At his hotel, Luke ignored his messages and stretched out on the bed, the air conditioning cranked up. He wasn't sure where Jesse was staying, but he liked to think that he was just a floor or two away. That Jesse was thinking of him, too.

"Jesus!" Luke shook his head. Next he'd be writing poems in his diary or composing sappy love songs. He popped a sleeping pill and got into bed, willing his mind to turn off.

Instead, he dreamt of running with Jesse on the beach, sand flying behind them, the water cool on their feet. He tripped, stumbling to the sand. He kept trying to get up, but his leg didn't quite work. He seemed to be in a perpetual loop, unable to rise and still not sitting comfortably. When a noise in the hall woke him, Luke lay awake, unsettled.

The next morning he felt sluggish and continually a step behind. He still pulled out an easy victory against the young qualifier, years of experience coming into play as he went through the motions.

On his way through the players' lounge, Stein Koehler greeted him with a smile and a gleam in his eyes that put Luke immediately on edge.

"Great match today, Luke."

"Thanks," Luke said, a fake smile pasted on his face.

"Your next match should be...*interesting*." With another smile, Koehler was gone, his hangers-on in his wake.

Outside in the main lobby, a huge board listed all the players in the draw and kept track of how the tournament progressed. Luke had been so preoccupied that he hadn't checked who his second-round opponent would be. He scanned the board quickly, finding his own name in a few seconds. In another second, his stomach plunged. He knew the name of his next opponent very well.

Jesse McAllister.

CHAPTER SIXTEEN

L UKE TRIED TO get in some practice but couldn't stay focused. Instead, he went to the hotel gym and tried to lose himself running on the treadmill, his iPod playing loudly in his ears. Of all the times for him to play against Jesse! He could already see the headlines, hear the giggles and whispers.

Over a hundred men in the draw, and he had to face Jesse. If it had been a month or so earlier, at least they would be talking about it. Luke wasn't sure whether he should call him, or not say anything until they met in the locker room before the match. Really, what could he say? They both wanted to win.

Someone had to lose.

He had just finished up on the leg press when Mike walked in. Luke gave him a wave and a tentative smile, which Mike returned. Yet he stayed on the other side of the gym and didn't look Luke's way again. Luke tried to go back to his workout, but after a while, he gave up.

Luke picked at his chicken breast dinner and half-heartedly pushed his food around his plate until there was a knock at his door. He opened it to find Mike in the hallway.

"Mike." Luke couldn't hide his surprise.

"Hey. How's it going?"

"Fine. Well, not really, but you know." Luke shrugged.

"I was just around and I thought…"

Luke motioned over his shoulder at his room. "You want to come in?"

"Sure."

"Want something to drink? Beer?" Luke opened the minibar, feeling strangely nervous. He and Mike had hung out a million times before, but everything was awkward and strange now.

"Sure, beer would be great." Mike pulled out the desk chair and sat down.

When they both had drinks, Luke perched on the end of the bed. "So..." He had no idea what to say to his friend of over ten years. "Great match today, taking Southard in straights."

"Yeah, thanks." Mike took a sip of his beer. "You didn't look so hot. Your serve was pretty weak."

"You're telling me." He and Mike had always been honest with each other, and Luke felt a strange sense of relief in the fact that some things hadn't changed. "I'd better get my shit together or I'll never get anywhere near the final."

"First you'll have to win your next match."

"Yeah." Luke wasn't sure what else to say. There was a lot he wanted to say, but would Mike want to hear it?

"It must be hard. Playing him. Jesse."

Luke kept his eyes trained on the carpet. There was a light stain near the bottom of the TV stand. Looked like soda, maybe. "Yeah. It's going to be hard."

"I thought he'd be here; I didn't want to...interrupt."

Luke's smile twisted. "No worries on that count. We broke up when I got back from London."

"Oh. Sorry to hear it."

"Are you?" Luke was genuinely curious.

"Yeah, I am. You were really happy there for a little while. I haven't seen you like that in a long time. Not since before Nik died. And maybe even not then."

"Yeah." Luke swallowed the lump that was rising in his throat.

"The last time we spoke it…didn't end so well."

"Oh. So, you haven't talked to him yet about this? About playing each other?"

He shook his head. "Not really sure what to say. I mean, it's a match, just like any other. One winner, one loser. The end." Except it wasn't just like any other match, and Luke knew it.

"It's hard enough playing a friend in a Slam, let alone…let alone your…well, I guess he's not your boyfriend anymore."

Luke drained the rest of his beer and laughed hollowly. "Nope, I guess not."

"So…why'd you break up? I mean, you were so happy there for a while."

"You really want to hear this?"

Mike smiled, and Luke could see the nervous tension there—but also the sincerity. "Yeah, I really do. Look, I've acted like a real jerk this summer. I always thought I was a pretty liberal guy, but it freaked me out more than I thought it would. I'm sorry."

"It's okay. As long as things can go back to the way they were. No more weirdness?"

"No more weirdness." Mike raised his bottle and Luke knocked it with his own. "Okay, so what happened with Jesse?"

"He wants to come out, tell the world we're queer."

"Whoa," Mike whistled. "That would make for a tough road on the tour. You'd have a hard time with a lot of the guys."

"Tell me about it." Mike understood, why couldn't Jesse? "And he's barely gotten started; he'd be screwing himself over for nothing."

"Well, not for nothing."

"What do you mean?"

Mike shrugged. "I can't imagine what it's like, pretending to be someone you're not. Being honest would be damn hard, no doubt about it. But maybe it's worth it in the end."

"Easy for you to say." Luke knew he sounded bitter, but he

couldn't help it.

"Yeah, I guess it is."

"I didn't mean to…I'm really glad you're here, Mike. I could really use a friend right about now."

Mike looked at him evenly. "Well, you've got one." The moment stretched out between them and Luke felt the lump rising in his throat once more.

"Thanks." After a moment, he slapped his knees. "How about another beer?"

Mike nodded. "Sounds like a plan."

Luke twisted the tops off the bottles and for the first time in weeks, he didn't have to fake a smile.

LUKE WAS ONLY at the National Tennis Center for about five minutes the next day before he ran into Jesse. An older couple and a young woman were with him, and Luke realized with a sinking sensation that they were Jesse's family.

Jesse froze in his tracks for a second when he saw Luke and Mike coming towards him, but then kept walking. His family noticed Luke as well and didn't bear the most friendly expressions.

"Hey." Jesse nodded as he passed Luke and Mike.

"Hey," Luke replied quietly.

"Is that all you have to say?" Jesse's sister glared at Luke.

Jesse turned around and sighed. "Caitlin, don't."

"Why not? I think the coward owes you more than that," Caitlin spat.

"I…um…" Luke stammered, his face suddenly flushed.

"Come on, Cait. This is none of your business." Jesse tugged on her arm.

"Well, I think your sister's right." Jesse's father's voice was low and steely. He narrowed his eyes at Luke. "So you're the man who beguiled my son and then left him a distracted mess."

"Dad!" Jesse stared at his father, open-mouthed.

"Well, it's true, dear," Jesse's mother piped up.

Jesse pointed towards the exit at the end of the hall. "Go, all of you." When they started to argue, his jaw clenched. "*Now.*" They complied reluctantly and shuffled off, casting a few glances over their shoulders as they went.

Jesse smiled weakly and glanced over at Mike, standing a few feet away. "My family's crazy. Don't listen to anything they say."

"It's okay, he knows." Luke glanced up and down the hall, but for the moment, they were still alone.

Jesse's eyebrows shot up. "He does?"

"Yeah, he does."

Mike cleared his throat. "Uh, maybe *he* should leave you guys alone. I'll meet you on the court, Luke."

Luke nodded, and Mike went down the hall. Luke knew other people would be along any minute, so he got right to it. "Look, we need to talk." He reached out for Jesse's forearm, the feel of his skin electric beneath Luke's hand.

"About what?" Jesse's tone was measured and indifferent as he pulled his arm out of reach.

"What do you think? About our match tomorrow."

"What's there to say, Luke? We have to play each other. So we will. One of us will win, one of us with lose. The end. Life will go on."

"So that's it? It doesn't bother you?"

Jesse exhaled. "Of course it bothers me," he whispered. "But there's nothing we can do about it. Therefore, we'll go out, we'll play, we'll shake hands at the net, and we'll pretend that we don't care. That it's just another match."

"Right." Luke nodded. "We won't give them anything else to gossip about."

Jesse's eyes narrowed. "That's all you care about, isn't it? Your precious reputation."

"No, of course not! But you just said—"

"Don't worry, Luke, I won't embarrass you. I won't make a scene." Suddenly there was a shout of laughter and voices coming from around the bend in the hall. "I'd better go; you wouldn't anyone to see us talking, now would you? I mean, what would people think?" Jesse's words dripped with cynicism.

"Jesse…"

But he was gone, quickly out of sight as some other players rounded the corner, talking animatedly amongst themselves. Luke quickly hurried to meet Mike on court. Once there, he tossed his bag down and pulled out a racquet, examining the strings closely.

"So…how'd it go?" Mike asked, tentatively.

Luke waved his hand dismissively. "Let's get working. We've only got the court for an hour."

Mike nodded and didn't press the subject. They rallied back and forth, and Luke tried to clear his mind, concentrate only on the ball. After dumping his forehand into the net for the third consecutive time, he threw his racquet across the court, the loud crack only making him feel worse, not better.

THE NEXT MORNING dawned hot and muggy once more, with barely a breeze coming from any direction. Luke was already sweating as he walked onto court, and he hadn't even played a point yet. Some dark clouds were moving in, but so far there had been no rain.

In the locker room, Luke and Jesse had barely looked at each other, just gone about their business and suited up. Since it was still early in the tournament, there were plenty of guys coming and going, so at least there hadn't been any awkward silences to navigate.

Out on the court, they warmed up together, as all players did before a match. First, they rallied back and forth lightly, forehands and backhands, maybe some volleys. Then they each picked a side of the court and warmed up their serves. After five minutes they were ready to play.

The chair umpire came out, and Luke and Jesse stood on opposite sides of the court at the net as the coin was flipped. Jesse won the toss and elected to serve first, as most players did. Only those with particularly strong return games would choose to serve second.

As they took their positions on court, Luke glanced around the stands. There were more people than usual for an early-round match on a Wednesday morning. He tried to brush it off, but he knew most people were there to gossip and speculate about his relationship with Jesse. To watch closely to see whether there was any truth to the rumors.

Shaking his head, Luke bounced side to side on his toes, trying to loosen up as Jesse got into position to serve. As they began playing, Luke tried to clear his mind, to forget that it was Jesse across the net. To forget that all he really wanted to do was take him in his arms, taste his lips again.

"Out!"

The lineswoman's call brought Luke back to the present. He'd just lost the first game at love, Jesse winning all four points easily. As Luke motioned to the ball boy for a ball, he tried once more to clear his head. He needed to concentrate if he was going to win this match. If he was going to beat Jesse.

It was Luke's service game, and he won, although Jesse got two points. The first set continued in similar fashion, Luke unable to keep his focus, unable to take control of the match as he should have been able to. He couldn't stop thinking, couldn't stop remembering.

Suddenly Jesse had a break point, and if he won it, he would be serving for the set in the next game. Big, fat drops of rain had started to fall, and the court was becoming slick. Luke looked to the chair umpire, but no call seemed forthcoming, so he served the next point. His first serve went squarely into the net and he cursed under his breath. The second went over, but he knew it was out just before Cyclops, the automated machine that bleated when a serve was beyond the line, sounded.

Double fault.

With the break of serve for Jesse, the umpire called a rain delay as thunder cracked overhead and the rain intensified. Grounds crew scurried this way and that, pulling down the net and covering the court as quickly as possible. Jesse and Luke both crammed their belongings in their bags and jogged off the court into the tennis center.

They silently made their way back to the locker room, which was teeming with players now that the rain delay was on. Luke went to the bathroom and decided to head to the lounge to find Mike. He was still at the sink when Jesse suddenly appeared.

Jesse didn't look at him, just concentrated on washing his hands. "Stop it," he hissed.

"Stop what?" Luke didn't look at him either, just took another dollop of soap and lathered back up again.

"You know what! Stop letting me win."

"I'm not," Luke whispered.

"Bullshit. I don't want your fucking pity, Luke. Or whatever it is."

Luke glanced in the mirror to double check that no one else had entered the bathroom. "I don't know what you're talking about. I'm just having an off day." But maybe it wasn't true. Maybe he didn't want to beat Jesse, didn't want to knock him out in the second round of a Grand Slam.

"Fine." Jesse looked at him in the mirror and their eyes met. "But if I'm going to beat you, I want it to be fair and square.

Okay?"

Luke nodded and Jesse turned on his heel and left. Luke peered into the mirror. If he didn't beat Jesse, that would mean he was out. That would mean Luke would lose what was probably his last real chance to win the U.S. Open.

Jesse was right. It was time to play the way he knew he could. No matter who was on the other side of the net.

IN THE ANNOUNCER'S booth, Steve Anderson whistled softly. "Rossovich's serve was up over one hundred and twenty miles an hour and McAllister probably didn't even see it going by. Another game to Ross."

As they went to commercial, the producer gave Steve some notes and statistics to talk about during the next segment. It was clear Luke Rossovich was going to win the match and he'd taken his next potential opponent to the cleaners every time they'd met, so he was looking good to advance to the second week of competition.

The players took the court again and Steve cleared his throat. "Well, Luke sure has come on strong in this match and he's looking in good shape. That rain delay did him a world of good; he's only lost three games since and it looks like he's going to take this match in straight sets."

His fellow commentator made a joke about what Luke ate during the delay to put the zip back in his step and Steve chuckled dutifully. "Well, whatever it was, he should stock up. It was a bumpy start, but his focus is back now and if he keeps it up over the next few rounds, he's on track to meet Riel in the semis and then possibly Koehler in the final. Of course, that's assuming both those players get through their rounds, too."

On court, Luke and Jesse slugged it out from the baseline

before Luke tapped in a beautifully placed drop shot to win the point. "With touch like that, Rossovich is going to be hard for his next opponent to beat.

"And Luke's got the break again here and the chance to serve this match out. Jesse McAllister didn't play badly, but he was just outmatched here today once Luke got the ol' engine in gear. But Jesse is certainly a young player we're keeping our eye on, he's had a great year and could be cracking the top fifty next year."

A few points later, and Luke had won the match. The two players jogged to the net and shook hands, exchanging a few friendly words. Steve and his partner looked at each other with raised eyebrows. They'd been given strict instructions from the producers not to mention the rumors that had dogged Luke and Jesse since London.

"Looks like these two players are still friendly, even though they're not playing doubles anymore. They sure did make a good team, and we're not quite sure what happened there—they really seemed to be jelling together."

In his ear, the producer shouted at Steve to change the subject. "Anyway, it's on to the next round for fan favorite Luke Rossovich. Coming up next is Taylor Vargas, a promising young American woman we can't wait to see in action."

They went to commercial once again and Steve smirked. "How much you want to bet Rossovich and McAllister are kissing and making up right now?" He and his partner laughed, and the producer chimed in with another lecture on keeping the broadcast family friendly.

LUKE'S HAIR WAS still damp from his shower when he headed to the pressroom to answer the obligatory questions. The hallway was empty, and Jesse stood outside the door, shoulder leaning against the wall.

Clearing his throat, Luke said, "Hey."

"Hey." Jesse didn't look at him.

"How's..." Luke trailed off. He knew how it was going. Not too damn well. "Are they backed up in there?"

"Yeah, that cute little Russian girl beat Pinneo. They'll be drooling all over her for a while longer, I expect."

Luke nodded and the silence stretched out. Finally, he said, "I'm sorry."

"For what?" Jesse faced him, arms crossed. "For winning? That kind of attitude won't get you to the final."

"For everything."

Sighing, Jesse leaned back against the wall. "Just don't, okay?"

"Okay." Luke shifted from one leg to the other restlessly. He wished they would hurry up and just get on with the press conference for their match already. "Going home tomorrow?"

"No, I'm still in the doubles."

"Doubles?" Luke felt gut-punched. "You're playing doubles? With who?" How did he not know this?

"With Logan Adams."

Tall, dark, handsome-as-hell Logan Adams? "Oh, since when?"

Jesse looked at him as if it was the stupidest question he'd ever heard. "Since a few days ago when the tournament started."

"Right." Luke fiddled with the label on his water bottle, pulling it off in strips. "So what's he like?"

"He's cool. Has a great backhand volley."

"What about off the court?"

"Off the court?"

"Yeah. You guys hanging out, or whatever?" The paper peeled away from the bottle and he stuffed it in the pocket of his shorts.

Jesse sputtered in disbelief. "Are you...are you *jealous?*"

"What? No!" Luke's face flushed and he knew he was as transparent as Saran Wrap.

Jesse looked quickly over his shoulder and then past Luke down the hall. "You are! You're jealous." He laughed and shook his head.

"I was just making conversation." Luke's jaw set and his tone went cold. "Forget I asked."

"Luke."

"I said, forget it."

Sighing, Jesse leaned back against the wall and stared down at the floor. After a moment he asked, "Would it matter if I was? Sleeping with him?"

The door to the pressroom opened and a perky woman burst through. "I'm so sorry for the wait, gentlemen. Who would like to go first?"

Since Jesse was closer to the door, Luke motioned to him and Jesse went inside, smiling and making small talk with the press officer. When it was Luke's turn, he took his seat and answered questions, laughing off the rumors about Jesse and steering the questions back to his game, to his odds of winning the tournament.

Luke could give the appropriate answers in his sleep. While he assessed the draw and his chances against the two men who were currently playing to be his next opponent, his thoughts drifted.

"Would it matter if I was? Sleeping with him?"

Luke was on his way to possibly winning his fifth Grand Slam and the coveted U.S. Open title that had barely eluded him years before. Jesse's question tumbled over and over in his mind.

Nothing seemed to matter quite as much.

Luke blinked into the lights high above the court and wiped his forehead on his sleeve as the crowd hooted and hollered and cheered him on loudly. The U.S. Open was the only Slam with night matches, and the New Yorkers who came down after work to watch were one of a kind.

The air was thick with humidity, and Luke's skin was slick and flushed. He'd only been playing for twenty minutes and he already wanted a shower. His road to the semis had been easy after beating Jesse. He hadn't dropped a set since, and with the break of his opponent Riel's serve, he was on his way to taking the first set of the match.

After a sleepless night, he'd managed to channel all his need and desire and longing for Jesse into his game. The thought of Jesse with anyone else was unacceptable, and the only thing Luke could focus on was the ball, the court, the chalk lines that made up the sum of his world until he played his last point.

He bounced the ball twice before tossing it up into the air and slamming it over the net. Most players had their routines and Luke was no different. Two bounces and then up. No more, no less.

Riel got his racquet on the ball, but it bounced harmlessly out of bounds. Luke felt like he was untouchable, like there was nothing Riel could possibly do to beat him. Koehler was through in the other men's semi, and Luke was on a mission to take him down in the final.

He motioned for a ball. Two bounces. Over the net. Riel barely even saw it as it zoomed by, just catching the outside line of the service box. The crowd roared, and Luke smiled to himself as he returned to his chair, another game closer to his goal.

CHAPTER SEVENTEEN

S TANDING IN THE tunnel that led to the court, Luke readjusted the bag on his shoulder and waited. The television crew was in front of the players, waiting to film their entrance onto Arthur Ashe Stadium. Seating twenty-three thousand, it was the biggest tennis venue in the world and the din of the crowd above pumped adrenaline through Luke's veins.

Beside him, Stein Koehler waited, his expression impassive, calm. He had smiled icily in the locker room and Luke had smiled back. They both knew that this wasn't just about winning a Slam.

This was personal.

An official waved them forward and the players walked out onto the court to the sound of thunderous applause. The late-afternoon sun was still high in the sky, and Luke couldn't see a single cloud. No breeze wafted by, and he already felt sweat on the back of his neck. Although he wasn't sure if that was due to the heat or nerves.

Luke sat in his chair and unpacked his equipment. He'd tried to plan the day perfectly—practicing a bit with Mike in the morning to stay loose, eating at the right time to give him energy but not fill him up. It was a delicate balance.

Mike had been eliminated in the third round but had stayed on at Luke's request. Luke footed the hotel bill, knowing that Mike couldn't afford to stay in New York City for an extra week when his daughter needed new braces.

The night before, Arnie phoned and wished Luke well, telling him that if he took the title, there were two new endorsement opportunities in the works. Good old Arnie, always with his eye on the prize.

Stephanie flew in the day before, greeting Luke at the hotel with a hug that lasted a long time. He'd grown taller than his mother when he was only thirteen, and Luke had to stoop to hug her properly. However, he didn't complain. Aaron arrived with her, and Luke was grateful to have another friend around.

Dinner with his mother, Aaron, and Mike had been quiet, and no one had brought up Jesse, for which Luke was grateful. He knew Jesse had only made it to the quarters in the doubles and had probably headed home days ago. Luke tried not to miss him desperately.

He didn't succeed.

As the crowd buzzed, Koehler took his side of the court and Luke took his time moving to the baseline. They warmed up, hitting the ball back and forth lightly. On one backhand, Koehler smacked it hard, and Luke returned the favor. A murmur rippled through the fans and a smile tugged at Luke's lips. It was going to be one hell of a match.

Luke was certainly right, since almost four hours later, the match was still going. After Koehler took the first set, Luke had won the second and third, only to have Koehler win the fourth. They stayed neck and neck in the final fifth set and went to a tiebreaker. As Luke wiped the sweat off his brow and stretched his left hamstring gently, he was thankful that one way or the other, the match would be decided soon.

His body had taken a beating and he wasn't as agile as he had once been. His knee ached, the joint protesting every time he came to a sudden stop or made a quick turn. He just needed to hold on for a few more minutes. Just needed to win a few more points.

As the clock marked four hours and one minute, the cheer of the crowd was like a wave of thunder crashing repeatedly on a beach. Breathing hard, Luke walked slowly back to the other side of the court. His legs felt like lead and his lungs burned as he gulped in the early evening air. This was it. Just a few more points.

Concentrate.

Ten minutes later, it was 5-6 with Koehler a point up. Luke didn't have enough gas left in the tank to keep going. *What kind of attitude was that?* His inner voice sprang to life. *It ain't over 'till it's over.*

With a deep breath, Luke nodded to the ball girl and caught the ball she tossed. He knew the crowd was cheering for him, trying to spur him on, give him strength. He bounced the ball once and caught it again before tossing it aside. He nodded for another, killing time trying to get his second wind.

Scratch that. More like his tenth.

Twenty-three thousand people held their breath as he bounced the ball twice and tossed it up into the air, his racquet catching it in the sweet spot and hurtling it over the net. There it skidded off the back of the service box and out of Koehler's reach.

The crowd exploded. It was 6-6. They switched sides and Luke served again, dumping the first one into the net. The second wasn't hit hard, but he managed to get a sharp angle on it and Koehler's smashed return went *just* wide. The serve went back to Koehler, who took his time setting up. Not that Luke was complaining about the chance to take a few more deep breaths.

The umpire shushed the audience and Luke bent into position, waiting for the blur of green fuzz to hurtle towards him. When it did, he returned it with a backhand down the line. Koehler smashed a running forehand crosscourt and Luke raced towards it, the ball moving faster than his legs could. He took a futile stab at it and tumbled onto the court.

As the crowd gasped, Luke rolled onto his back. The sky above was a dusky blue, the clouds reflecting the orange glow of the sun as it descended. He felt the roar of the fans vibrating through the ground beneath him and he slowly got to his feet. Millions of people were watching all around the world, and Luke felt like they were all there in the stadium, their expectation hot on his face.

He brushed himself off and the cheering intensified. Luke tried to soak up the energy, let it seep into his bones, his muscles, his skin. Suddenly the screen of the electronic scoreboard high above the court came into focus. Luke saw the camera zoom in on his mother in the crowd.

Yet Luke's gaze wasn't on her, but the person standing behind in the entranceway to the first level of seating. Almost out of frame, his arms crossed over his chest, lips pressed tightly together the way they did when he was nervous. A second later he was gone, the camera sweeping by on its way to check in on Koehler's latest supermodel girlfriend, who was poised as always for the camera.

Jesse had only been on screen for a few seconds at most, but he was unmistakable.

Luke was rooted to the spot. Jesse was here. He'd stayed. The image played over and over in Luke's mind as the crowd chanted and cheered and rose to their feet. Despite everything that had happened, Jesse was there. Jesse wasn't afraid. In that moment, Luke knew that he'd been wrong all along—Jesse didn't need his protection.

Luke gazed around at the pandemonium and felt a calm float over him, settling down softly like a veil. Win or lose, he knew what he had to do. For Jesse. For himself.

The umpire asked for quiet and for play to resume as Luke took his position on the court to receive serve at 7-7. Luke had a feeling Koehler would serve out wide. When he did, Luke was ready and placed his crosscourt return perfectly, catching Koehler off balance.

The crowd went wild, still on their feet and now making even more noise, although Luke wouldn't have believed it was possible.

"8-7," the umpire intoned. "Match point, Rossovich."

Luke took a deep breath and motioned for a towel, wiping his face quickly. At the service line, he held the ball in his hand and closed his eyes briefly. In that moment, he thought of all the years that had come before, of his father, of Nik, of Jesse. He exhaled and gripped his racquet, the ball bouncing onto the court. "One more point," he muttered.

As the ball flew up into the air, Luke's racquet met it and sent it speeding over the net. Koehler stabbed it back and Luke cracked a forehand up the line. Koehler was there and the ball returned once more, Luke running towards it and hitting it deep, near the baseline.

Koehler got it back but Luke was ready at the net, his volley arcing perfectly into the empty court before him. The ball hit the ground and sailed on as Koehler raced towards it. He pulled his racquet back and swung, the ball pinging off the frame and bouncing out of bounds.

"Game, set, match—Rossovich."

As the crowd exploded, Luke felt a huge weight lift from him as he thrust his arms into the air, his head tipped back, a shout of joy surging from him as he sank to his knees.

He was U.S. Open champion.

By the time Luke opened his eyes again and focused, Koehler was waiting at the net. The court was hard beneath his knees, but Luke barely noticed as he got to his feet and moved forward in a daze. The players shook hands, Koehler's tight smile insincere, his grip slippery. "Maybe next time, Stein," Luke said, before turning to the chair umpire and shaking his hand as well. Cameras were watching, and Luke would wait until later to tell Koehler to go to hell. On the other hand, maybe he wouldn't bother.

As Luke turned to wave to the crowd, thousands of flashbulbs exploding, Koehler didn't seem important anymore. Luke peered around at all the anonymous faces, thousands of strangers celebrating his triumph.

In that moment, there was only one person he really wanted to share it with.

To the consternation of the official who approached to discuss the awards ceremony, Luke darted away towards the stands, climbing over the barricade and into the seats, squeezing past spectators who clapped him on the back as he passed. He made it to the stairs and started up towards the first landing, a cameraman desperately trying to keep up.

Luke was pretty sure he had the right section since he'd seen his mother's ticket that morning, but in a stadium as huge as this one, he couldn't be sure. The faces he passed were a blur, the noise of the crowd rumbling in his ears until he couldn't even hear himself breathe.

Then he was there, his mother, Mike, and Aaron smiling and pulling him near for a group hug. He kissed his mother and wiped the tears from her cheeks, and Mike slapped him on the back before hugging him again, Aaron close behind.

Stephanie looked over her shoulder and Luke followed her gaze to find Jesse on the landing, hovering near the exit. As Luke walked towards him, Jesse's eyes grew wide, and he looked around uneasily.

People all around were cheering and clapping so loudly that Luke couldn't hear what Jesse started to say. Then their lips met and there was no need for words. Luke's hand slid behind Jesse's head as the kiss grew deeper.

He felt more than heard the gasp of the crowd, a shockwave that washed over them as Jesse pulled him closer, their mouths still moving together. Taking in a shuddering breath, Luke leaned back and looked into Jesse's eyes, his palm on his cheek.

"I love you."

Jesse smiled tremulously. "I love you, too." He kissed Luke tenderly. "Even if you are a slow learner."

Laughing, Luke wrapped his arms around him, lifting Jesse off his feet. A small ripple of applause broke the shocked silence that had settled over the crowd, and as their lips met once more, Luke realized that it wasn't a dream.

He'd just won the U.S. Open.

This was the title he'd wanted for so long. Somehow, it didn't seem nearly as important as the fact that Jesse was back in his arms, warm and soft and *his*. He'd just kissed the man he loved in front of everyone he'd been hiding from.

"I guess I'd better go get that trophy before they decide to give it to someone else."

"I guess so."

Luke leaned down, his lips near Jesse's ear. "Although I've got half a mind to just skip the ceremony and take you back to my room. Or to the nearest bathroom stall." He smiled when he felt the tremor move through Jesse's body.

"It'll be worth the wait." Jesse smiled wickedly and a bolt of desire coursed through Luke's veins.

"Damn right it will be." Luke glanced around at all the watching eyes. "Okay, I'd better go before we really give them a show."

Jesse squeezed Luke's hand tightly. "It'll be okay."

"I know." To his surprise, Luke realized he really believed it for maybe the first time in his life.

"I guess we're in for a wild ride, huh?"

"Yeah, seems like. But we're in it together."

Jesse grinned. "Don't make me cry, everyone's watching."

"So let them watch."

Luke leaned down and kissed Jesse once more, slowly and deliberately. With one more squeeze of their hands, Luke headed back down to the court, grinning at his mother and friends as he passed, the eyes of everyone in the stadium on him. The cameraman was close behind, another waiting for him at the bottom of the stairs. Luke knew the clip of him running into the stands to kiss his boyfriend would be a top story around the world, and instead of feeling afraid, he felt proud.

A few boos contested the smattering of applause from part of the crowd, but most of the audience stayed quiet aside from a low buzz of whispering. The tournament officials and sponsor representatives waited on the court, which had been set up for the awards presentation. The line judges and ball boys and girls all formed an honor guard of sorts, standing in even rows. Everyone on the court looked shell-shocked, as if Luke had just murdered someone in cold blood before jogging back to collect his trophy. The tournament director cleared his throat awkwardly as Luke and Koehler took their places.

After the director made a strained speech thanking the sponsors, he introduced Luke as the new U.S. Open champion. Beside him, Koehler sneered with disgust, which only made the grin on Luke's mouth grow wider as he hoisted the trophy high above his head.

EPILOGUE

S TEVE ANDERSON TOOK a quick sip of water as Jesse McAllister motioned for a ball. "Here it is, double match point for McAllister."

Jesse served, the ball flying up before he hit it over the net, perfectly placing it so the ball skidded up off the service line. His opponent stabbed at it, sending the ball into the net harmlessly.

"He's done it! Jesse McAllister is Wimbledon champion!"

As Jesse sank to the grass, the crowd leapt to their feet, cheering loudly. Jesse, looking slightly dazed, seemed to take a few seconds to let it soak in before standing up and waving to the fans. He shook hands with his opponent and the chair umpire before letting out a great whoop of delight.

"This is Jesse's first Grand Slam title, and you know he's been dreaming of this his whole life."

The camera cut to the player's box, where Jesse's family stood cheering, Luke and Stephanie at their side. "There are his proud parents, Bob and Julie; his sister Caitlin; and of course his longtime partner, Luke Rossovich, and his mother. I know Luke's been a great mentor, and Jesse has said that he and Luke still play doubles together whenever they get the chance."

As Luke embraced Jesse's mother, Steve went on, "Hard to believe it's been almost three years since Ross retired after winning the U.S. Open in most memorable fashion. It hasn't always been easy for them, but Jesse's shown here that he's got the talent to match the press coverage."

Jesse jogged across the court. "Looks like McAllister's going to do a repeat of Rossovich's performance at Flushing Meadows and…yep, there he goes up into the stands!" When Jesse launched himself into Luke's arms, most fans cheered and Steve couldn't help but smile.

As the network went to commercial, Jesse and Luke kissed joyfully, oblivious to the world around them.

BONUS EPILOGUE

I T WAS LATE by the time Luke and Jesse made it back to their
hotel. After showering off the red clay streaked across his body
from his victory tumble onto the court, Jesse had done hours of
interviews with the world media. Then, of course, it had been
time for dinner with family and friends at one of the finest
restaurants Paris had to offer.

Luke was more than ready to have Jesse all to himself again,
and he tried not to let his impatience show as Jesse's parents said
an extended goodbye in the hotel lobby. Luke's mother had
already gone up to her room with her boyfriend, Harry.

Harry was an accountant who made model airplanes in his
spare time and always smelled vaguely of glue. Luke teased him
mother about finding the most boring man in America to fall in
love with, but he was thrilled to see her so happy.

Once Jesse's parents were safely on the elevator, Jesse turned
towards the other wing of the hotel, his arm wrapping around
Luke's waist. "You up for some more celebrating?" Jesse whispered, giving Luke an exaggerated wink.

Luke's cock twitched just thinking about it. With Jesse focus-
ing on the tournament the past two weeks, the only sex they'd
had, a few days before, had been rather rushed. "Oh, I'm up for
it." Luke stopped and steered Jesse towards the front doors of the
hotel. "But not here."

"What, you're going through an exhibitionist phase? That'll make for some great headlines tomorrow."

Even though they'd been out for four years and most people were accepting—especially the people who mattered—Luke was still cautious. "No, we're going to our room."

"Uh, that would be upstairs."

"That was our old room." Luke smiled in what he hoped was an enigmatic way. "We're staying somewhere else tonight."

Jesse grinned delightedly, and Luke's heart skipped a beat. Jesse was twenty-seven now, but still hadn't lost his boyish enthusiasm. Luke was thirty-eight—pushing forty, as his trainer Aaron liked to remind him when they got together for their weekly session—but Jesse kept him feeling young.

A car was waiting for them, and they wound their way through the streets of Paris, the old buildings rushing by as the Lexus made its way along the narrow streets. When they arrived at their destination, Jesse's smile grew even wider. "The George V? You got a room here? Seriously?"

Luke simply winked in return and tipped their driver before getting out. The doorman ushered them inside the beautifully appointed lobby, and a woman appeared as if out of thing air. "*Bon soir*, gentlemen. Jean-Paul will show you to your suite." A man had also materialized, and he led them to the elevator.

Once upstairs on the top floor, Luke tipped Jean-Paul and shut the door to the suite. Jesse turned in a slow circle, gawking. "And I thought the Hilton was nice. Holy shit, Luke. This room must cost a small fortune!"

"Good thing you just won the French Open."

At the reminder of that afternoon's victory, Jesse beamed. "Yeah, good thing. It's also a good thing you got that job with ESPN."

Luke rolled his eyes. "Please, I do sixty-second how-to tutorials on improving your strokes. It's not like I'm a commentator."

"Not *yet*. But you will be." Jesse noticed the private terrace and opened the doors wide. "Oh my god! Have you seen this view?"

Luke had inspected the room a few days earlier, and the incredible view of the Eiffel Tower had sold him on it. The bathroom overlooked the city skyline as well, and the accommodations were luxurious in every way. Overstuffed cream-colored chairs and pillows with gilded accents made the rooms resplendent.

Standing behind Jesse on the terrace, Luke wrapped his arms around Jesse's waist. "Not bad, huh?"

Jesse sighed contentedly. "Not bad." He turned in Luke's arms and pressed their lips together. "What's the bedroom look like?"

They made quick work of their clothes as they crossed the living room, and were naked by the time Luke pressed Jesse down into the soft mattress in the golden bedroom, the duvet tossed aside. Their kisses started out playfully, but soon their tongues were demanding, breath coming in short gasps.

Jesse arched up, rubbing their hardening cocks together. "I missed you so much," he muttered.

"I've been here the whole time." Luke pulled back, catching his breath, a smile playing on his lips. "But I missed you more."

Jesse's arms wrapped tightly around Luke's back. "Sorry I've been so distracted."

"It's safe to say your distraction paid off."

The infectious grin was back. "I won. I can't believe I actually *won*."

"Just trying to show me up as usual."

"That's right. Next time we get in a fight I'll be sure to remind you that there's only one French Open champion in this relationship."

They laughed and kissed again, bodies moving together, skin soon becoming slick with sweat. Luke moved lower on the huge bed, his lips marking his path down Jesse's body. He took Jesse's cock in his mouth, making Jesse gasp with pleasure. Luke took him deeper into his throat, wrapping his hand around the base of Jesse's cock as his head bobbed up and down. When he knew Jesse was getting close, Luke pulled back, his tongue making one last sweep around the tip of Jesse's cock.

Jesse panted. "God. *Now.*"

Wanting nothing more than to plunge deep inside him, Luke cursed himself silently for not getting the lube out of his suitcase ahead of time. He slid off the bed and was back in a flash with the slim tube. Kneeling, he slicked himself as Jesse watched hungrily.

As Luke lifted Jesse's legs to his shoulders, Jesse pulled him down for a kiss. "Fuck me," Jesse gritted out, his teeth pulling at Luke's lip. Then there were no more words as Luke thrust inside him in one swift motion. The heat was intense, the feel of skin on skin almost enough to bring him over the edge. They hadn't used condoms for years now, and trusted each other completely.

Luke only started moving when he was back in control, the feel of Jesse tight around him making his whole body tingle with pleasure. Sometimes he marveled at how he could still want Jesse just as much now as the first time they'd met. Jesse's body was as familiar as his own now, the taste and smell and feel. In the past, he'd wondered if they'd ever get bored with each other, but Luke never stopped wanting him.

They moaned in unison as Luke rocked in and out, Jesse's head thrown back on the pillow, his mouth open. "Oh god, Luke. More."

Luke pushed into him over and over, pressing Jesse's knees against his chest, opening him up further. Jesse's cock was hard and leaking, trapped between their bodies. Fingers tight in Luke's hair as he kissed him again, Jesse took in a ragged breath. "Harder. *Harder.*"

His muscles beginning to strain, Luke grunted with each

thrust. When his balls tightened, Luke reached between them, squeezing his hand around Jesse's cock. He pulled in unison with the motion of his hips, and Jesse came, the liquid heat splashing up onto their chests. As Jesse shuddered with release, Luke emptied inside him, a long moan escaping his lips.

Luke was barely able to whisper Jesse's name before collapsing on top of him. Jesse's legs slid off Luke's shoulders and they both tried to catch their breath. Beneath his ear, Luke could hear Jesse's heartbeat slowly return to normal.

Lifting his head, Luke lazily swiped his tongue over Jesse's stomach and chest until he was clean. "If you're hungry, we can order room service." Jesse teased.

"Well, there is a bottle of champagne and dessert in the living room."

"Do you think if we call, someone will come up and bring them in here?"

"The service *is* supposed to be impeccable."

Jesse laughed. "We'd have to give the guy a pretty big tip." He wriggled his way out from under Luke. "You stay and rest, old man. I'll go."

"Hey, who said I was old?" Luke turned onto his side and propped his head in his hand. He watched Jesse walk into the other room—or more to the point, he watched Jesse's firm, round ass.

"You say you're old every time I beat you on the court." Jesse popped a strawberry in his mouth after putting down the tray laden with fruit and chocolate on the bed.

"I still win my fair share of matches."

"Mmm hmm. Hey, we're playing doubles at that charity thing next month, right?"

"Damn straight. Stein Koehler is going down."

"Not that you hold a grudge, or anything."

Luke affected an innocent expression. "*Moi?* Never."

"He's playing with Riel. It's not going to be an easy match."

"But it's a match we're going to win."

Jesse chuckled. "Glad to see your competitive juices are still flowing."

"Oh, my juices are flowing. Don't you worry about that."

Jesse nipped at Luke's neck. "I have no worries."

"Speaking of flowing liquids…" Luke reached for the champagne. Once it was poured, they raised their glasses and clinked them together lightly. Luke cleared his throat. "To the new Roland Garros champion."

"I will never get sick of hearing that, just for the record." Jesse took a gulp of his champagne.

"Soon to be Wimbledon champion for the second year in a row."

Jesse snorted. "Not if Chernekov has anything to say about it. Or Richardson." He took another big swallow, and Luke mused that Jesse would be drunk before long, since alcohol always went straight to his head and the wine had been flowing at dinner. "Is it wrong that I don't even care right now about winning Wimbledon again?"

Barking out a laugh, Luke shoved a piece of cantaloupe into Jesse's mouth. "Get back to me when we're in London and you step out onto the grass again at Queen's Club. You'll be raring to go for Wimbledon."

"I know, I know." Jesse flopped back onto the bed, sending some strawberries rolling onto mattress. "It's just so hard to go right from clay to grass. Thank god I have a bye in the first round. Maybe I should just skip this tournament and rest up for Wimbledon."

"I think you know what Jeff will say to that suggestion."

Jesse sighed. "I think it would involve something about not resting on my laurels."

"He's a great coach, and he'd be right. You don't have to win

Queen's Club; just play a few matches to get ready for the big show. But you don't have to worry about that tonight."

"You're right, I don't." With quick movements that scattered more fruit every which way, Jesse took Luke's glass of champagne and rolled him onto his back. He straddled Luke's hips and tipped the cold, bubbly liquid onto his chest. Luke barely had time to cry out before Jesse's warm mouth covered his nipple, sucking it gently.

Jesse took his time lapping up the champagne from Luke's skin, and when he was done, Luke was hard again. Jesse grinned. "So, how private is that terrace?"

"*Very.*"

"Hmmm. It's such an incredible view. Would be a shame to waste it." Jesse leaned down and kissed him.

"Especially since it's our last night in Paris."

Jesse disappeared into the bathroom and came back with two robes, tossing one at Luke before slinging his over his shoulders. Luke followed him outside, closing his eyes and taking a deep breath of the warm night air. The lights of Paris spread out before them, the Eiffel Tower rising up towards the sky.

Flowers bloomed in every corner of the terrace, their sweet fragrance lingering in the air. The balcony railing was wide, and Jesse spread his arms out, bracing himself. Luke reached down and lifted Jesse's robe, his fingers making light, teasing circles over his skin. He whispered in Jesse's ear. "Tell me what you want."

"You. Your cock inside me."

Luke continued making light strokes over Jesse's skin, his fingertips skimming over Jesse's nipples and down over his stomach. A soft breeze whispered over them, and Jesse shuddered, goose bumps rippling over his skin under Luke's hands.

"Do I have to beg?" Jesse's eyes had drifted shut.

Taking hold of Jesse's hips, Luke inched his way inside him. "You might have to."

Jesse pressed back, trying to take more of Luke in. "You just love being a tease."

THEY BOTH LAUGHED, and with a sudden movement, Luke pushed in to the hilt. He took Jesse's earlobe between his teeth. "Open your eyes." Jesse did as he was told, and Luke began moving his hips back and forth slowly. "Get a good look at your kingdom."

"I'm king of the castle." Jesse giggled softly and then moaned as Luke hit just the right spot.

"That you are." Luke pulled out and thrust back in, hitting the sweet spot again. "I'm so proud of you." He reached down and caressed Jesse's cock languidly. "So proud."

Jesse turned his head and captured Luke's mouth with his own. They kissed gently at first, but soon their tongues dueled, and Luke increased the pace of his thrusts as he stroked Jesse harder.

They came almost at the same time, and afterwards they finished the champagne on the terrace, watching the twinkling lights of the city until their eyes grew too heavy.

AS THE SUN'S rays began to brighten the room early the next morning, Luke thought about getting up, but burrowed back into the sheets instead. He heard Jesse in the bathroom, and figured he had another twenty minutes at least to sleep.

Then the mattress dipped. "I know you're awake."

Luke kept his eyes shut and made a noncommittal noise.

"Have you seen the size of the bathtub? Come on, let's try it out."

"Five more minutes."

Jesse laughed. "You always say that! Your idea of five minutes and the universe's are not the same." Regardless, Luke heard him leave.

A moment later, he was back. "Did you know this is the honeymoon suite?"

At this, Luke opened his eyes. "Hmm?"

Jesse, wearing his robe, sat cross-legged on the bed with the bill that must have been pushed under the door, enclosed in an embossed folder. "Holy crap, this really was expensive." He leaned down and kissed Luke softly. "It was a great surprise. Thanks."

"Anytime. Anytime you win a Grand Slam, that is."

"Great. No pressure!" Laughing, Jesse went back into the bathroom. Luke heard the water turn on, and the tub begin to fill. He waited. Jesse should be poking through the tray of fancy salts and bubble baths—he loved that stuff.

Less than a minute later, Jesse was back. This time he held a small velvet box in his hand, and he looked back and forth between it and Luke. He opened his mouth, but only managed to get out, "Wha…?"

"Cat got your tongue?" Luke's heart began pounding lightly in his chest, and his mouth was suddenly dry. What if this had been a bad idea?

Jesse knelt on the bed beside him. "Luke, is this…? Are you…?"

Taking the box from Jesse's hand, Luke opened it. Inside were two white gold bands. "I thought maybe it was time. I know we're already committed, but I just thought it would be nice to make it official. Well, as official as possible considering we can't legally get married. Yet." Luke realized he was starting to ramble, and stopped.

"I don't know what to say."

Say yes. "It's okay if you don't want to. It was just an idea." Luke's face flushed.

Jesse blinked in surprise. "Why wouldn't I want to?"

"I don't know; I don't want to pressure you." Luke sat up against the pillows and tried not to fidget.

The seconds ticked by as Jesse watched him, a smile finally dawning slowly on his face. "You really think I'd say no?"

"I...I don't know. Does that mean you're saying yes?"

"Of course I'm saying yes, you idiot."

The relief had barely set in before Jesse practically threw himself into Luke's arms. They kissed and laughed, everything else forgotten as they explored each other, hands and mouths roaming, bodies straining together. Jesse was sucking enthusiastically on Luke's cock when Luke suddenly realized that the sound that had faded into the background was the water still running in the bathroom.

They spent the next ten minutes mopping up the bathroom floor with every available towel, and Luke prayed that the water hadn't seeped into the room below. He wondered what kind of insurance his credit card had, and whether it would count flooding one of the most expensive hotel rooms in Paris.

Then they dug around in the sheets for their rings, which had been flung aside when Jesse accepted the proposal. Luke found one near the foot of the bed and lifted it up triumphantly. "With the luck we're having this morning, maybe you should put this on for safekeeping."

Jesse was lost under the bedding, and popped up a moment later, the other, slightly bigger ring in his hand. "Not a bad idea."

Taking Jesse's left hand, Luke slid the ring onto his finger. Jesse did the same with Luke's ring, smiling widely. "I love you."

Luke kissed him, and murmured softly. "I love you, too." He couldn't imagine his life without Jesse. Hoped he never had to.

When Luke woke again a couple of hours later, the sun was much higher in the sky. He knew they should get up and get ready to travel to London. Start the whole process of trying to win a Grand Slam tournament again: warm-up event; media interviews;

working out and practicing on a precise schedule. He'd done it countless times over the years, and Jesse would do it countless more.

Jesse snored lightly, his breath warm and wet on Luke's neck. They really should get up—the real world was waiting. Instead, Luke closed his eyes and held Jesse tighter as he drifted back to sleep.

Just five more minutes.

The End

About the Author

Keira aims for the perfect mix of character, plot, and heat in her M/M romances. She writes everything from swashbuckling pirates to heartwarming holiday escapism. Her fave tropes are enemies to lovers, age gaps, forced proximity, and passionate virgins. Although she loves delicious angst along the way, Keira guarantees happy endings!

Find out more at: www.keiraandrews.com

Made in the USA
Columbia, SC
15 July 2022

63533348R00117